That Church Life 2

Teresa B. Howell

SPECIAL DEDICATION

This book is dedicated to my mother,
Helen Jean Richardson Ellis.
Rest in Heaven.

CONTENTS

That Church Life 2

ACKNOWLEDGMENTS

I am thanking God once again for the awesome support from family, church family, and friends. I never dreamed that book one would make such an impact on so many people but I am grateful. God is good and He gets all the glory, honor, and praise for my talent.

To my mom, Helen Ellis, and my grandmother, Era Ellis-I miss you dearly and I hope I made you proud. R.I.L.

To my dearest Calvin: I am so blessed to have you in my life. Your unconditional love helped me to stay on track. You are truly the love of my life. I love you!

To my children: You allowed me to write and understood the process. I love you Calvin James, Leondray, and Nephew/Son

Joshua. Thanks for putting up with me over the years.

To my mother-in-law, Rose C. Howell: Thank you so much for inspiring me to write. Your push put it all in motion. I love you!

To my daddy, James M. Ellis: You continue to make me laugh with your corny jokes. You give me material to write about and you don't even realize it. LOL... Love you!

To my father-in-law, Calvin Jr.: You are a true book salesman. Thank you so much for spreading the word. Love You!

To Carli, Cora, Jala, Nae, Daja, and even Madison: Thanks so much for your love and support.

Being an only child of my mother was rough, but I am thankful for all my sisters and brothers from my dad who embraced me with this book and during my time of grief: Jayme, Valerie, Marsha, Ashley, Anthony... Love you!

To Cheryl Smith Ellis-My listening ear: Thank you for being there for me when I needed you the most.

Marlana, Margaret, Marcus, Dorothy Edwards, Bettye, Ieena,

and Ann: You all allowed me to cry and get it all out. I love all of you. Tiffany, Nikki, Charnai, Tatiana, Erica, Brian, Jackie, and Aunt Doris… You are the family that will always show up and show out. I love you!

To Pastor Irma Berry Scott: You are a true sister indeed. Thank you for your love and support.

To the Victorious Ladies Reading Book Club in Durham, NC: What would I do without you? Meeting such a positive group of ladies is a true blessing.

To the editors that contributed. Thank you for all your hard work!

To the Ellis, Richardson, Howell, and Howard family… I love you! To Peace Baptist Church Book Club in Raleigh, NC, Radiant Readers in Mississippi and the Barber family: I'm so thankful for how you spread the word, passed the book around, and encouraged me to continue writing. All those late-night text messages to help me through… wow… I will never forget how you helped me.

To Mr. Roger Echols (District attorney) and Laura Echols:

Wow, the two of you are amazing with big hearts. Thanks for all your assistance with research.

To Holloway Funeral Home: Never met funeral directors who keep you laughing and help you sell your book. What an amazing group of folks. Feel free to bury me when it's my time. LOL.

To Heather Butler and the Butler Literacy Agency: Your advice in the beginning of my journey helped me tremendously. Thank you for calling all the bookstores and putting my name on the map.

To my Aunts: Janice Woods, Michelle Kallie, and Beverly Howell: Thank you for supporting me at the events in your area, and listening to me babble about my book 24/7. You allowed me to run my mouth and you never said, "Enough about That Church Life!" I love all of you!

To Mt. Olive Holy Church (Durham, NC), Victory at Calvary (Durham, NC), Faith Assembly Christian Center (Durham, NC), Gateway to Heaven (Durham, NC), Greater Walton UHC (Durham, NC), Calvary Temple (Oxford, NC), Mt. Calvary Living Word (Burlington, NC), Overcomer Ministries

(Kernersville, NC) and St. James Baptist Church (Henderson, NC), Mt. Calvary (Roxbury, Mass) and New Mt. Calvary Greater Worship and Praise Ministries (Dorchester, Mass) … the list goes on.

Bull City Pitmasters… thank you for always feeding me!

Diamonds Literary World, Diane P. Rembert, Robert White, Cyrus Webb, Lissha Sandler, Shawnda Booklover, and Ella Curry… the best promoters on the planet.

To Brian Schneider (my white brother from another mother), your technology assistance at a drop of a hat has been priceless!

To Maurice Scriber and Rebecca Pau, thank you for fulfilling those late night graphic requests at the drop of a hat. You two are my saving grace!

If I have left anyone out, charge it to my mind and not my heart. Thank you to all the churches listed and not listed for the support of my books. I am honored and humbled.

May God bless each and every person that touches this book.

ONE

MICHELLE

This just happened...

While looking over at all the blood on the floor, I desired a normal life. With the little bit of strength, left in me, I grunted. I fell against the wall while trying to catch my breath. Sweat poured from my neck as my breathing intensified.

Heavy winds pressed against the window. The local news stated earlier that a level two Tornado was expected to touch down in the city of Durham during the evening rush hour, but the storm was the last thing on our minds.

The troubled man with bloodshot eyes changed our lives forever when he walked into this room with a bat and knife. Now he was dead, his remains saturated with his own blood.

Several voices echoed around me.

I tuned them out. My focus was on the body on the floor

wrapped in the curtains that used to adorn the windows in this room.

The knife was still in my hand, the nine-inch blade pointing to the floor and dripping blood.

I burst into loud sobs.

I repositioned my body against the wall, sliding downward. I pivoted my feet sideways and gazed at him. His eyes were still open with dried tears on each side of his face.

I'm a faithful churchgoer. I pray often. I read the Bible daily. I love people. How did I lose control?

"God help us," Natalia said as she placed her hands on her face.

For several years I struggled; coping with life's challenges alone. Don't know how I survived it all as most women would have given up by now. So many hidden secrets were buried inside me. It became difficult to hold information away from my best friends, Missy and Natalia, as my lies became more and more convoluted. Pastor Jones was the only person other than my mother who knew all the details.

A lot of emotions festered as I jabbed the knife at him. *I lost it. A few hours ago, I'd told Missy that Tommy raped me and now this?* My instinct tells me that I'll have to be brave enough to tell the truth of it all. *I'm so not ready.*

"It's okay sweetie. It's going to be okay," a trembling Missy whispered.

Natalia stood there crossing her arms and rubbing her hands against them. She hadn't mumbled a word. I suppose she was in shock.

I looked down at my clothes. Blood was smeared across my breast, all over my arms, and down my pants legs. I could feel the eyes of Missy and Natalia burning through my chest as they stood motionless in front of me.

I shifted my eyes, scanning my wrist and forearm. My skin peeled from carpet burns formulated in the struggle. Warm, stringy blood strands splattered around us. I'd created another crime scene in the pastor's study, and it was ten times worse than the first one.

I observed the room.

And there it was, the one thing that I was desperately trying to avoid, Missy's eyes—eyes that were filled with venom. It was heart-breaking to see them filled with liquid and agonizing pain.

I stood up and moved in closer, hovering over his body. We all stood side by side, staring down at his corpse. Pastor Jones lay nearby, still unconscious from the bat that went across his forehead when Tommy walked in.

I felt myself leaning over. I replayed what happened over again in my mind. Then I felt something touch me. For just a brief moment, peace filled the room. It was as if his spirit was floating above our heads.

Missy reached over and grabbed me, holding me close while her tall, lanky body towered over me. I cried like a baby. With all that had been said and done, it was now obvious to all...

I Michelle Hanks, murdered Tommy Lee Davis with his own knife.

Beanie called the police and in no time, the paramedics, men in blue uniforms, and CSI rushed in. They checked the pastor, he was still breathing. When they reached Tommy, they checked for a pulse and found nothing. He was gone.

I can't believe I just killed this man.

I was remorseful. I pulled back suddenly covering my eyes standing and filled with embarrassment. I became inaudible as a clear line of urine trickled down the back of my legs.

"What are we gonna do, Missy? What are we gonna do?" I screamed as a faucet of tears plunged down my face.

TWO

MISSY

*Daddy groaned, holding the top of his head. He shuffled his feet, trying to get up. Beanie helped him from the office floor with one hand.

I could see the pain seeping out of Daddy's eyes while struggling to stand. He wobbled to the wall with blurred vision, squinting after every step. He looked as if he was trying not to cry.

"I need all of you to leave the room now," said a heavy-set paramedic with a deep voice. He was dressed in white and followed Daddy into the hallway to examine his head. We all shuffled behind him.

Daddy braced himself as the man's big hands tapped around the knot on his wrinkled forehead. "Hold on sir. Give me a minute," he whaled, not wanting to be touched.

"Sir, please let me help you. Pastor Jones, right?" The paramedic asked, "Say your full name."

"Henry Jones is the name. Now let me be. I'm just fine." He winced.

I looked over, releasing a long sigh of relief once Daddy responded to the calling of his name. But I couldn't seem to hold it together any longer. I marched around with Beanie moving quickly behind me for support. Natalia stood beside Daddy, monitoring his every move as Michelle stood in front of the office door frozen in a daze.

Daddy hobbled over, reaching for my hand. "Let's go get some fresh air, baby girl before your anxiety starts acting up. Don't you all worry about me." He looked into my eyes. "I'm okay, gal. *Really, I'm okay* and we gonna make it through this."

We moved slowly outside, colliding into the fast winds and cold air as we watched additional police cars pull up closer to the church walkway.

A police cruiser and an unmarked car parked in front of us.

A short, stubby man jumped out of the unmarked car with enthusiasm. He wore a brown suede suit jacket with matching loafers standing around 5'3. When reaching the walkway, two other men in uniform joined him.

He cleared his throat and used his hands as a megaphone. "Greetings everyone. My name is Detective Cooper. I was nearby and I heard the call about an altercation. Is everyone okay?"

ı "No sir," I replied with a runny nose and cascading tears. "Our musician is dead."

"Your musician?" His eyes widened, "Oh, I see. Where did this happen?"

Natalia stepped forward. "In the pastor's study."

"Alrighty then. I was given some preliminary information when I agreed to answer the call and I will proceed with the questioning."

"Yes sir, we understand how it goes. Our backup musician, Michelle is inside also," Pastor Jones replied. "She's trying to get it together. Just give her a minute."

The detective paused, looking down and reading information from his phone screen. Then he moved his head back up and gave the ground rules. He raised his arm in the air as if he was a basketball coach trying to get his team's heads in the game. "Alright, listen up. I just got the official word. The tornado is approaching in this area within the next hour. I will be moving quickly. It has touched down over on the other side of town and the roads are blocked. But I need you to understand, my questioning takes precedents over the weather. Rain, sleet, snow, or shine. I need everyone to cooperate. Got it?"

We all exchanged looks of bewilderment. My feet pitter-pattered on the pavement as I felt lightheaded.

"I am going to take a look at the crime scene inside and then I will call each one of you one by one for questioning. No talking to one another, no walking around without an escort, and no disappearing acts. Understood?" He pulled out an iPad mini and a stylus pen from his coat pocket to take notes.

We all nodded in agreement.

My face burned in humiliation. I didn't want to go through all of this.

The detective bent his head down with his partial bald spot glistening in the light. He walked inside as we remained outside with one of the blue uniformed participants. He returned whispering to the officers and then looking over at my tear-blotted face with curious eyes. "Since you spoke up first, what's your name ma'am?"

I swallowed deeply. "Missy Rochelle Jones." I croaked the words out and immediately regretted that I hadn't kept the anxiety out of my voice. I was ready to be that little girl running track again. I wanted to run far from all of this. But this time, I remained in place while my daddy patted my back. The others walked inside with the officer. They had looks of concern.

I couldn't move even if I wanted to my feet felt like they were stuck under a pile of rocks. I took deep breaths, trying desperately to stay conscious. The trees around me seemed to be moving closer. I blinked several times to get the pool of blood surrounding Tommy's body out of my head.

"What's wrong with her?" He asked my father.

"I'm sure she wouldn't want you to know all her business. You might want to say what you need to say while you got the chance, sir. She's going through something."

"Well, whatever she's going through, you can't continue to stand out here while I question her. Please go back inside," the detective blurted.

Daddy walked back toward the building. He had the *I trust God* stare in his eyes as he shuffled his feet slowly. I couldn't figure out if he was moving slower than a turtle due to pain or due to sheer uneasiness. Either way, I wanted him right beside me.

Detective Cooper took his advice, talking so fast that I started having trouble understanding him. He ran through a series of other questions, which included my address and telephone number before asking, "And who are you in relation to the deceased?"

I trembled at the word *deceased* with water trickling down my nose. "He was my boyfriend of five years. We broke up several weeks ago."

"So, tell me, Ms. Jones… may I call you Missy?" The detective asked, moving his stylus pen in the air.

I didn't respond.

"So, tell me what happened?"

I didn't answer. I fumbled with my hands and tapped my feet. He looked down, then back at my facial expression.

"How did Tommy end up dead?"

My feet tapped harder.

"Since you aren't willing to answer. Let me ask you this?" He lifted his iPhone again, reading notes and said, "What's your relationship to Michelle Hanks?"

I answered in fragments trying to keep a straight face. "She's… been a true… and faithful friend… of mine for many years."

"Hum, her name is mentioned several times in the CSI information texted to me. Was she the person who took him down?"

My tongue tingled. I could feel my eyeliner run down below my eyes. I wanted to say something to defend her, but I couldn't. *This can't be my life.*

I tried my best to answer the question, but after the third try, nothing came out. *My anxiety was exposing itself in ways that I couldn't control.* "I... I... I... don't... know... what... too say…" I tried to release the phrase *self-defense* mouthing the words, but it just wouldn't come out. I pulled my shirt to my mouth, biting on the fabric with a frantic attempt to gain self-control.

The detective flung his hand up and dismissed me, quickly losing patience with my unclear responses. "I'll come back to you in a few minutes. I don't understand what you're mumbling."

My words remained stuck in my throat. Whenever I was nervous, I was at a loss for words. The only time I didn't have this problem was when I preached God's word. I didn't care to answer any of his questions anyway, even if I had some form of control over my anxiety. All I wanted was to be near Tommy's body. I had to get closer to him. I had to lay on his chest one last time. I had to speak my peace into his ear.

I desperately longed to hear his voice and before I knew it, I let out a multitude of urges all at once as I cried, stomped, and cried again. I'd never get the chance to heal from our break-up.

The detective's eyes became bigger as he observed my behavior. I belched out a loud scream, rearing my body back with an attempt at talking to Tommy's spirit within the clouds.

"TOMMY! TOMMY!" I bent down grabbing the bottom half of my dress holding my knees.

"Ma'am, let me get you inside. You're losing your mind out here."

A police officer rushed over to the detective's side upon hearing my screams. Detective Cooper escorted me into the building, quickly locating an empty chair in the hallway for me. I plopped down right next to Michelle who looked like she was in zombie mode.

Overpowering dry coughs burned my chest as I tried to get it together. I didn't want Beanie, who was now my new boyfriend, to see me like this. But I just didn't know how to control it. I felt sleepy. My fight or flight strategies were nonexistent. Spasms began to shoot up and down my spine as I tilted my head against the wall. *I needed a healing for my soul.*

THREE

NATALIA

The clouds were pitch black, moving in circles, but despite the weather, the questioning continued. It was no rest for the shocked and weary defending victims of a brutal attack.

I stood outside, leaned back, watching the behavior of this overly zealous detective that stood in front of me. He seemed overjoyed at being the appointed person for questioning. He carried himself as if this was the first time he had ever been a part of something so major. He had the gleam in his eyes that reminded you of a college basketball championship fan watching the last video segment of one shining moment. I'm sure cases like this was what a detective lived for.

"State your name ma'am." "Natalia Freemon."

"Spell that last name for me, ma'am."

"F-R-E-E-M-O-N."

"Uh huh. I think I might know some of your kinfolks." I paused shrugging my shoulders.

His eyes sparkled while his voice escalated with excitement. "You're James Freemon's daughter, aren't you?"

I gave a slight nod.

"Well, I'll be darn," He uttered. "That's my homeboy from high school. Small world, isn't it?" He chuckled. "I used to play football with your daddy. Hillside High Class of 1958. Umm hum... We used to crack some heads back then."

I wasn't remotely interested in his inappropriate drift down memory lane. It was too cold out here for this. He went on and on with his story, ignoring my clear level of irritation.

"I knew your mama too. She was James's high school sweetheart from what I remember."

My eyes burned. Mentioning my mother at a time like this was a no-no. I stepped into the grassy part of the walkway, trying to calm down. I folded my arms tightly across my chest. The feisty spirit in me wanted to tag him. Instead, I recited the code of conduct learned from anger management classes.

Don't react to the misguided actions of others. Allow your actions to guide others to victory.

I took a deep breath as the cool air filled my lungs.

"Are you paying attention, Ms. Freemon?" I blinked away.

"Yeah, I hear you."

v "Was that your mama that James married?"

I was very sensitive to the fact of losing my mother in a car accident. After her death, I was left with my womanizing father, a long time deacon of the church. I blamed him for her death although he's tried to make amends over the years.

My mother was released from jail one cold wintery morning. Ice covered the roads that lead to the county jail. But that didn't stop her from calling a taxicab company to get her home. She wouldn't have dared ask my father to pick her up. She had called to let me know that she was on her way, but she never made it home. The 2007 yellow Volvo she rode in with a taxi sign on the roof, hydroplaned in the middle of highway 85, spinning onto the path of oncoming traffic. It was hit by an oncoming eighteen-wheeler which pushed the Volvo further down the highway, sending it smashing into another vehicle. She and the driver died instantly at the scene.

If my daddy lived right, she wouldn't have been in jail that weekend, locked up due to a domestic violence call from one of our neighbors. Apparently, one of daddy's women came to our home and approached her with the heartbreaking news that he was once again unfaithful. She'd been dealing with his infidelity for years and her rage commenced a butt whooping for my daddy and the other woman. Mama was short, but powerful when it came to sticking and moving. The more he cheated, the stronger she became.

While in flight attendant school, I became a die-hard advocate for domestic violence victims and women getting jail time for defending themselves. Watching this murder unfold shifted my mind back to my mother's situation. I did everything I could to protect my friends. I didn't want any women to experience such turmoil due to a man's indiscretion. This was probably why Missy kept stuff from me as much as she could. She knew I wasn't going to take being tagged by a man lightly. I was passionate about making sure that women have a voice and not a bruise.

The sad thing about all of this was that Michelle would probably go down for a crime when she was just trying to protect us from a foolish and jealous man.

Such an awful situation.

The last thing I need is being forced to listen to this detective babble. I wish I could just go back to work. Flying around the world was my escape from reality. I don't like feeling like this, and I don't like seeing my friends suffer either.

"Yes, that was my mother. Next question please." My eyes twitched from the dirt lifted high from the wind. The tornado was moving in closer and closer as tree branches swung around, detaching themselves from the push of the wind.

The detective gazed at the black clouds and said, "We need

to go back inside now. I'll get back to you and question the rest a little later. This storm is about to take us down."

When we walked back inside, Missy was standing in the middle of the hallway consoling Michelle and waltzing back and forth with a small bottle. She rubbed holy water on everyone's forehead, including her own while chanting, "Jesus, Jesus, Jesus." She interceded with the others as they were bending over to receive their dose of anointed liquid.

This was one of the tactics she used not only to get to Jesus but also, to slow her anxiety down. Instantly, she started praying with a hack in her voice, "Father we come to you right now in the name of Jesus. Jesus, Jesus, Jesus, Jesus." The words scrolled across her tongue faster than she could spit them out. Saliva leaked out of the corners of her mouth, splashing onto her cheeks.

"Lord help us right now, Jesus."

"Lord have mercy. Missy, I need you to sit your hind parts down somewhere. I'm already seeing yellow dots and you want to plead the blood. Jesus knows we need him right about now. Rest your brain, gal," Pastor Jones demanded as he scratched his beard.

Beanie looked over, his arms folded. He had this look of *what have I gotten myself into* on his face.

Missy ignored the comments and the stares.

"Come on over here, sis," Missy said, reaching her hands out as Michelle leaned in for comfort.

She leaned over into the crease of her bra sobbing uncontrollably becoming the catalyst of tears.

We all cried simultaneously.

Michelle looked up at Missy's grief-stricken eyes. "What did I just do?" she whimpered.

Traumatized was an understatement.

"You did what you always do," Missy responded. "You protected me in the midst of trouble."

The officer looked as if he were watching a sad movie. He delivered the message in a soft tone, "Quiet ladies."

Wet spots formed on the top of Missy's chest.

"I just want to go home!" Michelle's voice echoed.

I responded, "It's okay, sis. We'll get to go home soon, I'm sure." Deep down, I knew it wasn't guaranteed. "We need the paramedics to look at your arm. You're in bad shape."

A policeman stepped out of the office asking, "How can we contact the victim's family?"

Missy gave him a bewildered look. "We're considered his family." She put her head down as if reminded that Tommy was really gone.

Her sniffles became loud snorkeling noises. She let go of Michelle and walked closer to the office door, trying to look inside. It was clear, her crazy love for Tommy had manifested again in full force.

*We all inched behind her as the section of the hallway leading into the room was still blocked off. Nevertheless, we still had a clear visual through the glass parts of the office door.

I peeked around the doorway to look for myself as the paramedics were called over to examine Michelle's arm. Tommy's body remained in the same spot. He was no longer pale looking. His body pigmentation turned back to its normal color and his hands were placed in front of him.

Dead at the tender age of twenty-nine.

But one thing was for sure, the tormenting, lies, hits, and the verbal abuse would no longer hinder Missy's ministerial growth. Although she might not realize it yet, Missy was finally free to be the woman of God she was called to be.

I've always wanted this for her; to be fearless while preaching God's word. My goal as her friend has always been to push her to greatness. Missy had the potential to be the next Joyce Myers. She also had a family tradition to uphold. No man should have that much control over a woman to the point that she loses her identity. I was going to make sure she accomplished her goals with God no matter the obstacle.

I held my breath with my hands pressed on my hips. I knew what was coming next. We looked up at the ceiling, amazed at

Teresa B. Howell

the sound of a downpour. Silent, we listened to rain hitting the roof with force.

20

FOUR

MICHELLE

The drastic downpour of rain didn't stop much. It was a true forensic showdown as the Crime Scene Investigators walked around taking notes, capturing evidence, and discussing their findings. *Law and Order* on Tuesday nights helped me understand their lingo as I watched them move around. Trails of blood crisscrossed from the study to the back door.

I'm am sure somewhere in the world there are church folks who don't have to go through all this madness.

Pastor Jones clasped his hands and said, "Now, I know Tommy's body won't be released from the medical examiner for a few days but we need to sit down and talk about how we're gonna handle this man's funeral?"

"Funeral?" I mumbled, putting my head down.

"Yes, Chile. I know this seems like a bad dream." He spoke

in his preacher's voice, chomping his jaw around. "Does he have any living kinfolk? Cause if he doesn't, I'll call Pastor Jenkins from the main church to do the eulogy."

"The last thing we want to talk about is his funeral arrangements, Daddy," Missy said, slumping down.

"Well, we got to do something, gal. They gonna take this man's body out in a few. Does he have any family to call and tell them that he's left this world?"

"He has a brother," I answered.

Missy looked up at me with a look of *who asked you* and said, "I'll get his brother's number from my Rolodex once they let us back in the office."

"A brother? Are they tight?" Daddy asked with his face scrunched. "I never knew he had a brother."

"Yes, his brother Arnold lives in New Jersey. They grew up in Bragg Town."

Daddy scratched his head. "Well, glad to know he has someone to handle all of this. I hope they got life insurance on him. You know black folks don't always insure their kinfolk. You got life insurance, Beanie?"

Beanie smirked at the question. "Yes, sir... I do."

"Well good. Just checking. I don't know how they do it in other countries."

Our eyes traveled when one of the investigation team

members came out of the office. Tommy's body could be seen in the background. He was packed inside a black body bag with a gold zipper. Three men stood beside the white gurney stretcher ready to transport. They rolled his body past us, pausing to check the condition of the gurney wheels that squeaked loudly.

Fierce winds slammed against the building.

ʳ"We might have to wait a few minutes for the wind to calm." The examiner said to his coworkers.

That might be a clever idea," Daddy said interjecting into their conversation. "God got that wind whistling at us."

"Can we see him?" Missy asked.

The bag was zipped all the way up to the top. "I don't think you need to see him, Missy," Pastor Jones said.

This did it for her. Missy had an anxiety attack. She shifted gears completely piercing her eyes and blowing out short breaths from her mouth while clawing at her chest.

I couldn't even fathom what she was going through as it became difficult to watch her transformation. Watching Missy suffer like this made me feel worse. I folded my hands together and prayed silently.

"Dear Lord, please give Missy the strength to make it through this. We need you right now Lord… And Lord, I am calling on you to give me strength as well. Despite it all, he was my friend. I never wanted to hurt

him like this. I can only imagine how bodies are stuffed in a morgue. Flimsy tags placed onto the big toe of the deceased. Skin tugged in every direction by the examiners. Blood all over tables. Bodies shoved around without knowing who loved them last or who will miss them the most. Lord, give us strength and forgive me for my wrongdoing."

Missy ran toward the stretcher. She bent and pressed down on the bag near his ears. "Tommy, if you can hear me, I want you to know that you're the love of my life. I will always love you, no matter what we've gone through."

The medical examiner tried to move forward as his coworker pushed her aside. Beanie walked over and pulled her away gently, embracing her. "He can't hear you anymore, sweetie. Don't do this to yourself. He's gone on to be with the Lord."

She reached for the stretcher and plopped down, falling through his embrace. Her head landed on Tommy's chest. We tipped over to her side without saying a word. I continued to pray.

"I'm just sad right now; so very sad. Knowing that I will never hear you laugh again. Knowing that I will never see you smile again. I'm sorry, Tommy. I'm so sorry, baby. I'll miss you with all my heart. I'm so very sorry." Her tears became little puddles that splashed on the left side of the stretcher. "No baby, no. Don't leave like this."

Her cries magnified. She reached up pressing her palms

against her cheeks frustrated. Her eyes bulged as she rocked back and forth.

Then it happened again. She fainted.

Missy fell, hitting the ground hard.

Simultaneously, the tornado crashed down with a big bang vibrating the floor. The room became black.

FIVE

MICHELLE

The lights flickered back on as I opened her purse looking for medication. I didn't feel comfortable rifling through all her items but I had to help revive Missy from yet another attack.

She had several sermon topics scribbled on loose leaf paper. I grabbed a mini notebook fanning her back and forth. The anxiety bug had eaten her alive. I continued to fan. But yet, no response.

"Speak to me, Missy. Can someone help her, please!"

"Step aside ma'am. Let me look." The paramedic's jacket had the name Bob embossed on the chest.

"She suffers from anxiety and faints when she loses oxygen."

He moved to her other side listening for a pulse, checking vital signs. "Can you hear me, Missy? Squeeze my hand if you can hear me, please," Bob said, kneeling in front of her.

This is all my fault.

After several minutes of non-responsive behavior, Bob probed and primed her body in preparation for an IV with his burly hands.

"What are her vitals looking like? Is she going to be okay?"

Oh, God!

Cotton balls filled with strong smelling medicine were placed under her nose. She responded with a cough.

"I'm going to carry her into the other room. Should we take her to a hospital? What do you normally do when this happens?" Beanie had a million and one questions as he moved around the hallway.

I could only imagine what this was like for him. Here he was, visiting his new girlfriend in another country and was caught up in a murder. Black men didn't want this kind of drama—it didn't matter what part of the world they were from. Brothers knew if they were in the room with a corpse, someone was going to try to put that dead body on them. I could see sweat oozing from his pores.

"She's been hospitalized several times for fainting when she doesn't take her medication regularly. But since we have help right here in the building, they can handle it. She'll be fine. Let's all keep calm," Pastor Jones interjected. The cool timbre of his voice was no mask for the worry lines across his forehead.

Beanie gently picked Missy off the floor and kissed her on the cheek. His feet clanked hard against the floor as he moved with force. He carried her across the hall to Deacon Freemon's office with the younger Justin Bieber looking paramedic. Her IV bag dangled in the air.

Beanie didn't wait for the medical team to suggest the next steps. But who was going to challenge a tall, dark Jamaican man with bulging muscles?

I followed his footsteps as he placed Missy on the sofa.

Natalia cat-walked in, patting me on the back for comfort with a fake smile and strained cheeks. "It will be alright, lady. *Breathe.*"

I had mentally surrendered, dropping my hands in front of me. Apologizing publicly for my wrong wouldn't make a difference at this point.

Natalia gazed at me with a look of worry and grabbed my hand. I used the other hand to rub my belly gently feeling bloated.

"He's gone. He's really gone, huh?" I mumbled.

"Yes, he's gone, hon. We can't do anything else for this man. Missy needs us now."

His body was transported out into the medical examiner's truck. I hope there were some angels in heaven to greet his soul. I hope someone he knew came to the pearly gates saying, "Welcome home, brother."

I hope.

The only thing I had left.

Hope.

SIX

NATALIA

Beanie stood in the middle of the room monitoring the scene with a school principal's stare as Pastor Jones rested in a recliner, propping up his legs.

Detective Cooper made his way over holding his iPad up with both hands. "I didn't get everything I needed from all of you."

Then he looked directly at Michelle. "However, Ms. Hanks, you need to come with us."

My heart hammered against my chest.

Michelle looked at me with distressed eyes as if she knew what I was thinking. I had my advocacy group, *Black Girls Reign* on speed dial. We would march in front of the precinct if we had too. A black woman killing a man in these parts was a big deal. A little extra media with the group backing behind her wouldn't hurt.

"Do what they ask of you, Michelle. We have your back. Let me walk with you outside." I looked over at Detective Cooper and asked, "Can I speak with her alone before she leaves?"

The detective touched the nape of his neck and responded, "Say whatever it is you need to say with the quickness." The officers walked behind us. Pastor Jones and Beanie stayed with Missy.

Michelle and I fell into step together. She trudged down the hallway, smacking the hollow walls out of frustration. I'm sure the guilt alone made her spastic.

"Believe in God, Michelle. You did what you had to do. Once they get all their notes together, they'll understand that you protected yourself. And most of all, you protected us." I clenched her left shoulder with a supportive embrace.

Once outside, I paused from the strong winds. The storm passed, leaving trees and power lines knocked down, blocking the walkway, and part of the entrance.

The detective's decision blindsided me. I looked over the horizon pointing to the clouds and spoke with authority, "We have *Him* on our side. *He* has us all covered."

Michelle turned away. She didn't seem to have the comfort in God that she normally expressed. I used my index finger to form an imaginary cross against her chest, reminding her that she was a child of the Almighty. She was protected. Although folks viewed me as abrasive, my attitude never overpowered my love for Jehovah. She needed to know that God still loved her, despite what it looked like.

Two police officers walked behind us. "Michelle Laverne Hanks?"

She turned around, flailing at the wind. "Yes?"

"You have the right to remain silent. Anything you say can be held against you in a court of law. You have a right to an attorney…"

"She's just going down for questioning, right?" "Whatever they see fit at the precinct."

"It was self-defense for God's sake. She should be able to go home."

The officers ignored my request and kept walking.

I sped up behind them, determined to get my way. "Okay well, can I at least let the others come out and see her before you take her in?"

The officer paused and said, "Sure, do what you want."

I ran inside to tell the others as Michelle eyeballed the officers every move.

I came back outside with Beanie and Pastor. I wasn't good at praying so I needed pastor Jones to speak to the Lord on my behalf.

The police car was in motion with Michelle seated in the back. She looked back through the rear window.

"Wait, please wait," I shouted. "We didn't get a chance to pray for her."

Ignoring the plea, the officer continued to advance out of the parking area. *I pray that the District Attorney won't push this forward and arrest her. Lord, please let them just question her and send her home.*

I called the president of BGR, right where I stood saying, "Get the girls together. I think we need to help one of our sisters. I'll explain everything later."

SEVEN

MISSY

At the age of 9, I was baptized in a three-inch pool at the Victorious House of Prayer Holy church in Goldsboro, NC. My young preaching daddy put his large hands on my temple, allowing my long locks of hair to dangle down my back. His all white robe rubbed against my face as my anxiety grew. I was concerned about the large mass of water that would flow into my eyelids. I mentally tried to prepare the best that I knew how.

"In the name of the Father, in the name of the Son and in the name of the Holy Ghost." Daddy pushed my head downward while holding the arch of my back.

I slid deep down into the lukewarm pool of water in a long white dress, gasping for air. I didn't know how to swim at the time and wasn't given clear instructions on how to react while under either. Instead of holding my breath like most people, the water gushed into my nose and mouth. Large gulps of liquid sloshed around my throat. My arms flew straight up. I gargled while letting out a big gasp.

Daddy pulled me back up quickly, ending it with, "In Jesus name."
He dipped me a second time as if the first time didn't get the job done. I
was eventually pulled up from the pool of splendor as my daddy called it
while water continued to propel around me. I realized quickly while
overpowered by his strong grip, I had no control. I didn't have the strength
nor the might to stop the act of almost drowning. I couldn't express to
anyone that I needed help. I could only move my arms from side to side
hoping that my daddy would realize that I was in some form of danger.

It was the greatest form of desperation I had ever experienced. Those
same feelings came back time and time again, whenever I had bouts of
anxiety. This short-lived vulnerability was happening again at this very
moment.

I laid on the office sofa at Mt. Zion Holiness Church dazed,
and once again feeling powerless. Nebulous thoughts swayed in
my head with clear images of water splashing in my nose and
down my throat while I gasped for air. Every time I blacked
out, the haunting memories of almost drowning brought me
back to being nine-years-old again.

I sat upright on the plush blue sofa feeling groggy and
holding my head. Deacon Freemon's office was dissimilar to
mine. I liked purple while he was enamored with Duke blue. I
liked African American art while he was fascinated with sports
team's paraphernalia.

I gazed at the Duke University team pictures sprawled across the wall, but could barely see the player's faces. I blinked to gain my focal point and scanned the wall again. Deacon Freemon was a true Duke collector with over twenty-five pictures on display. Coach Mike Krzyzewski's photo hung in the center of the back wall surrounded by former Duke teams.

My vision clear, I noticed Natalia sitting beside me holding a cup of water in her hand and an expression of complete and utter disbelief. Her hair started frizzing, leaving her limp curls hanging over her ears. Hair moisturizer ran down the side of her face and her lip gloss had faded. She tried to play it off with a half-smile that didn't reach her eyes, but she looked exhausted.

"Here drink this, sis," she said firmly, shoving a cup of water into my hands.

"Thanks." I smiled and sipped slowly. My hands shivered.

Daddy looked over across the room rocking in his chair still holding his head.

"Daddy, you okay?"

"I'm still seeing stuff gal."

"Beanie looked outside the door to see if Bob was still on the premises. He yelled down the hallway, "I need some help in here."

Bob walked in with his partner with a quirky sense of humor. "Who needs help now?"

"My dad. I think he's ready to take a trip to the hospital. Right daddy?" I gave him a stern look.

Beanie sat up on the edge of the couch quietly right beside me. He was withdrawn from the conversation and seemed like he was ready to go.

"What's wrong sweetie?" I asked as the medical team prepped daddy for the ambulance.

"I can't believe you reacted that way when that man's body came out. I thought you were over him."

He held a sixteen-ounce water bottle in his hand, prepared to replenish at any given moment.

"I didn't have control of my thoughts, sweetie. I don't know how to describe it."

"I understand. But how do you think I am feeling right now? I didn't travel down the next road over to see your pretty face just to witness you falling out over another man. Maybe you're not ready to move on as my lady. Maybe…"

I stopped him by rubbing his arm and said, "Maybe I'll try a little harder next time. You're right. You've come this far to spend time with me and that's a blessing. I owe you some form of respect. I apologize, love."

"Exactly," Daddy responded while being prepped. "That's what I'm talking about. Put your foot down boy. She cut a monkey for that nut like he was gonna jump out of the bag and kiss her. He been treating her bad for years and she out here pouring out the waterworks over him. I hate to say it but, God sees and He knows…" Daddy stopped abruptly holding his head again as the paramedics shoved him onto the stretcher.

Beanie still seemed disappointed even after my apology. He leaned over as if he was gathering his thoughts.

I inspected the deep scar on my arm reminding myself of why Tommy was never good for me. It was a wound from a fight Tommy and I had a year ago. After all, I had been through, Beanie was right… how dare I still be thinking about my abuser.

"Stop!"

I balled my fist up tightly striking back at him as hard as I could. Tommy seemed to always find a way to make me show my cantankerous side. He continued to cheat and lie. We went back and forth, exchanging hits, moving left to right as my cat, Twinkles, bounced around trying to dodge us. He felt justified doing his dirt, and I felt justified when I aimed for his mouth each time I felt disrespected.

We scooted around from the kitchen to the bedroom and then back into the kitchen again. I wasn't going to stop hitting him until all my anger depleted. In other words, he was catching these hands until I felt better.

I reached forward smacking him dead in the mouth as he fell backwards onto the floor. Being a tall and skinny girl, I had uppercut advantages. I was strong as an ox, and I could always handle him. He was strong too.

But I didn't hold back. Breaking several objects, we tussled a'' around the tiny two-bedroom apartment on Duke Street with minimal wiggle room.

He threw his hands up ready to strike again as I ducked down. He pulled me up by my arms. I stood up straight as he got in position to hit me again. His hands mashed against my skin and I returned the sting with a few uppercuts to his face.

"I hate you!"

He paused with his eyes widened. "Well, if you hate me so much, why do you stick around?"

That was the million-dollar question I had been asking myself for years.

Why do I stick around to keep going through the drama with this man?

I looked up at him. I was still trying to catch my breath when I said, "Why do you stay? You can leave also, you know."

"That's the thing, Missy. I don't want to leave. You are my forever." When he talked like this in the past, I used to melt. But not today. Not after this fight. I looked down wondering about the case of Lorena Bobbitt who cut off her husband's body part and threw it in an open field. How could I make that happen? Where would I put it?

"You done?" he asked.

I nodded. I felt something shift in my soul. My head felt like it was about to explode. It was a lot of drama to handle.

"Oh, now you want to sit quietly and play innocent, huh? Don't start tapping your feet with your fake emotional issues now! And you better not tell your father that this is all me either."

Our eyes met for a moment. Was this negro lecturing me about my behavior?

He continued, "You are the abuser in this relationship, not me. Always trying to pop off over small stuff."

I rolled my neck. "Excuse me? So, you seriously think this is all small stuff? Stop sleeping around and we wouldn't have these darn issues. Learn how to control your little water sprayer and I will learn how to control my hands."

He shook his head and began pacing again.

"We are not married, Missy, so why can't you just chill? Technically in the eyes of God, I am still a single man."

I shoved my finger in his face. "What did you just say? You gotta be kidding me! Married or not, it's called respect honey. Aretha Franklin made that very clear and even spelled it out for negroes like you. I am tired of taking trips to the doctor to get medication for all the diseases you bring back to me. The man who claims that he loves me so much doesn't even respect me enough to wear a condom." I struggled to keep my emotions under control, but I couldn't win. I was too hurt.

Tears trickled down my face. I felt like a vein in my head was going to burst. The throbbing became more than I could bear as I put both hands on the side of my face holding my cheeks tightly.

Realizing there was no rebuttal after such a true statement, he continued to pace the floor. His energy was heavy with guilt, but like he always did, Tommy made an excuse. "I love you, Missy. I really do. But the problem is you spend too much time in church. You never have time for me."

I cast a glance sideways at him. He poked his lips out and pouted like a child not getting his way. It was not cute.

"So, now you gonna blame the church for cheating on me?" I threw my hands up. "You know what…you're insane."

He stopped pacing and sat down beside me. "I'm trying to tell you how I honestly feel, and you call me insane?"

I looked over squeezing my fist ready to strike again. "Missy, I don't do things to intentionally hurt you." "Whatever!" I hissed.

"Last time I checked, females are supposed to cook, clean, and look cute for a man, not throw punches. You're doing stuff that isn't considered Godly for a woman of your status," he said with sarcasm. "And you call yourself a preacher, huh? I know somewhere in the Bible it says that a woman should not raise her hand to her man? Got to be a scripture for this kind of mess."

I crossed my arms.

"What happened to just loving one another?" he asked.

I laid my head down on my bamboo memory foam pillow not wanting to entertain the conversation. I allowed him to ramble on as I closed my eyes trying hard not to respond. He undressed and put on the white t-shirt and basketball shorts he slept in. After which, he fell into bed right beside me as if nothing happened. He moved about, getting good and comfortable before leaning over and kissing me on my forehead.

"Can we start over?" he asked. "I don't want to fight with you

anymore. I love you, girl!"

I rolled over on the other side of the bed, scrambling for strength. I knew what was coming next. Sex. It wasn't going down like that tonight, or was it? I stared at the wall while wrestling between my flesh and common sense.

He tugged on my waist, trying to get me to face him. I just wanted to slap him one last time. "Yeah, let's start over. You can get your things out of my apartment and go back to your own place." I rolled over and pushed his hands away from my body.

"Keep your hands to yourself. If you find that to be a problem, you can leave right now." Our eyes locked and I saw shock in his. "I think that might be even better."

He growled, jumped up, and pulled his pants over his shorts. He pulled the keys to my car and apartment out of his pocket and tossed them on the bed. He walked to the door, putting his hand on the knob. Before he opened it, he did a half turn in my direction and said, "You gonna need me before I need you. Believe that."

I cocked my eyebrow.

"And by the way, the food wasn't all that great either. Rubbery chicken was never my thing." He left, slamming the door behind him.

The pictures on the walls clattered in the same rhythm as my heart.

I was a fool to stay as long as I did. I definitely had a touch of the battered woman's syndrome going on that I didn't realize until now. But it wasn't the time or the place as my new boyfriend did all that he could to make me happy over the last few weeks.

"I'm sorry, baby. Do you forgive me?"

Beanie crossed his eyes, still vexed.

"Let's just see how it goes from here on out me lady. We might need to slow it down a bit. I don't like competing with another man when it comes to my woman. I don't care if he is dead or alive."

It was time to pray and fast for some true deliverance because Beanie was the best thing that ever happened to me and I didn't want to lose him.

"You're right my love. It will never happen again." I bit my finger nails. *I will try and keep my promise. I love Beanie. Unfortunately, I am not in love with him just yet.*

EIGHT

NATALIA

We arrived at the hospital with Pastor Jones. After waiting around for hours, a nurse brought him back into the room. He received x-rays and CAT scans on his head. His results came back in a positive light but considering his age, he was probably going to stay the night for observation.

A fifty-five-inch plasma television with a "Duke" sticker was mounted on the wall directly in front of us as Pastor clicked on the remote control. He sat with his legs crossed in the hospital bed while flipping channels and stopping on WRAL, Durham's local news station.

A news flash appeared on the high definition monitor catching our attention. We stretched our necks outward, gawking at the screen. The church was in the background. They were reporting on what happened.

He turned up the volume once the words *breaking news*

scrolled across the screen. A blonde and gray-eyed girl standing in the front of the building holding a piece of paper with a microphone waiting to be cued in for the story. Her eyes zoomed straight into the cameras with the wind ruffling her white and baby blue jacket. The wind was still strong, it looked as if it was going to take her frail body up in the air. She tried to remain steady while pushing her blond-streaked and tapered hair out of her face.

◆Beanie pointed to the screen getting Missy's attention while she sat back nodding in and out. "They are outside the church. Look! Lord have mercy."

I hissed.

"I guess Durham don't play around when it comes to relevant and updated news," His mouth was wide open.

The entire crew of reporters, camera people, and a few locals stood on the side of the church prepping to go live. Missy appointed my father, Deacon Freemon to stay on the premises until the mayhem settled down. He stood beside the reporter looking into the camera. The onlookers and *Black Girls Reign* who were in the background made funny faces and flashed peace signs as they enjoyed being part of the media frenzy.

"Yeah, you don't have to worry about getting fake news in these parts, son. Durham reporters are always in the mix," Pastor mumbled.

———

"Good evening, John Baker here at WRAL coming to you with a live story. Our WRAL news team is on the scene of Mt. Zion Holiness Church on RTP Avenue located on the south side of Durham. The victim, twenty-nine-year-old Tommy Lee Davis was stabbed to death. WRAL's Christy Monroe is there with the latest details on the story." The reporter made minimal movement as he waited for the cameras to switch to the crime scene.

"Christy, are you there?" he asked.

"Yes, John I'm here. Mt. Zion is one of the largest churches in Durham and I stand here tonight gathering information. As you can see, there are still a few officers still on the premises."

Police walkie talkies echoed in the background.

The camera moved around the perimeter of the church parking lot, showing the landscape with crime scene investigators trotting up and down the walkway.

"Sources describe this case as a real-life *fatal attraction*. The victim apparently just couldn't move on after the recent break-up with the pastor's daughter."

Pastor flinched. "Lord God. They tell every cotton pickin' thing they hear, don't they?"

ꞌThe reporter continued. "Authorities are still investigating. This is a tough pill for the community to swallow, John."

"And wasn't this the same guy we reported on a few months ago after being shot in that same location?" he asked.

"Yes, it is."

"Well, I am lost for words on this one, Christy."

Pastor's feet thumped against the bed. "See, that's why I don't like watching the darn news!"

He lined the remote control to the cable box, attempting to turn the television off while the reporter said her final words. "This is Christy Monroe reporting live from Mt. Zion Holiness Church in Durham. Now back to you, John."

John shuffled back around to the camera tugging on his suit jacket. "We will have more on this story once more information is gathered."

Pastor jerked the remote, pressing the off button before slamming it down on the floor.

"We can't have no doggone privacy 'round here. *Jesus!*"

"It's the way of the world, I guess," Beanie said, shrugging his shoulders.

"Too much media and not enough praying in this world."

"You got that right, Pastor. I interjected. He was looking much better than when we first arrived. His hands started to move as he talked. That was a good sign that he was almost back to his normal self.

"Beanie, I need to do a background check on you boy. After all this, any man who breaths on my daughter is gonna need to have a full-fledged interview from here on out. My God."

Beanie chuckled. "Back home I was one of the evangelists for my church and on the Deacon board. You can check my references, I'm more than good these days."

Pastor leaned back, lifting a can of diet coke up to his mouth. He took a few gulps and said, "Well ain't that something. Missy got her a man in the church. Hot dog. It's a new day ain't it, gal? You dropped them zeros and got you a muscle-bound Jamaican hero."

We all laughed loudly.

"If it wasn't for Natalia, we wouldn't be together. Thank God for her offering me a free vacation." Missy reached over for Beanie's hand.

"Natalia always on the job. That's what I'm talking 'bout. We need more no-nonsense people in this world like you, Nat."

"I try to keep her straight pastor."

I'm shole glad to see those big pretty eyes of yours open, gal. You feeling better?"

"I'm okay… I guess," Missy answered.

"You still can't seem to get those loopy loop episodes under control. One day you'll get it right."

Beanie starred with a side eye. "Loopy loop? Is that what you call her attacks?"

Pastor smirked. "That's our code name for it. We've been calling it that since these darn things started."

"Oh." Beanie inched closer, rubbing Missy's leg.

"What else are you supposed to call it when your only child is falling out in public?"

"I just never heard the term used, that's all. Sounds rather insensitive, don't you think?" Beanie shook his head back and forth.

Pastor ignored the comment. "Oh, I forgot to mention, I've already called Pastor Jenkins to do the funeral. We got permission from the brother while you were under your..."

"Please don't say loopy loop out loud again," Beanie pleaded. Pastor rolled his eyes. "Now I like you boy. Don't mess it up." Beanie laughed. "I will try not to, sir."

"Anyway, don't you worry about nothing else concerning this. You hear, gal? The church got it all worked out."

I had a half smirk while listening to Pastor Jones jabber on and on. This is what we were used to—Pastor trash talking with his hands and mouth. He was on his way to recovery.

Missy sulked as if she was thinking about today's events all over again.

"I guess we should all just go home now. I need some time.

Just me and God," Missy said.

"Yes, we all need to rest. Pastor Jones, we will come and check on you tomorrow. Looks like you will be here overnight."

"Yeah, that's what it looks like, gal. Thank you all for being troopers. Lord knows today was the craziest day ever. I just hope they don't charge that gal. It's a sad commentary."

"She'll be fine. My organization is four thousand women nationwide. A man that beats on women and attacks the victim's friends was killed. That is what we're all about, protecting women that fight back."

Pastor Jones pumped his fist in the air signaling Black Power. "Never looked at it like that. I thought you all just liked to be seen on television." He chuckled. "You smart when you want to be, gal."

"Maybe if I would have called your group years ago, today wouldn't have happened," Missy said.

"You can't ask crazy why they crazy, gal. Whether you called that group or not, today would have still happened cause that boy was Koo Koo."

"Amen to that," I mumbled.

"Now move on with your life. You and Beanie make a nice looking couple. And he acts like he got some sense. Enjoy one another while he's in town you hear?"

"Yes sir, we will," Beanie responded, leaning over to put his arm around Missy. "She's been warned; once she gets that dude out of her head, we will be better off."

"I will be praying for just that Beanie. Who wouldn't appreciate a nice guy like you? Right, Missy?" *She didn't realize what she had. I wish I had a man like that. I might luck up with one like him from my online dating sites one day.*

She leaned over and kissed Beanie on the lips. "Right."

If he didn't say anything, she would still be sobbing in a corner somewhere like a basket case over Tommy. She ain't fooling nobody but Beanie right about now. Or was she?

NINE

MICHELLE

Late Saturday Night...

"Get me out of here," I yelled through the interrogation window.

I prayed that all of this would be over soon. My voice sounded from down the corridor of the police station as I remained isolated. The lights hanging above my head flickered, while the detectives walked back and forth.

I plopped down in the center of a chair with sweaty palms, full of nervousness. I glanced over my shoulder to view the dust all around the room. It was apparent that this particular interrogation space wasn't used often. The heat of the room created perspiration between my legs and damp sweat beads on my creased forehead.

↗ I wiped my lips, moving multiple layers of dry skin that dangled around the corners of my mouth. I was dehydrated and needed more liquids after sitting in the heat for hours. I leaned over sideways every now and again to vomit in the bucket that was provided for me. A vomiting spell started in the police car and didn't stop. It was something about the oppressing smells that curled my stomach. The odor reminded me of boiled minced meat that had overtaken the entire facility. I tried desperately to cover my nostrils with my shirt.

I contemplated on my future identity—my new misery and possibly the end of my youth. I didn't want to go to jail as fear became part of my being. I quaked.

After deep evaluation of the situation, I deemed killing Tommy necessary. He was going to kill all of us if I didn't take control. I saw terror in his eyes. He didn't leave me with many options.

Why would you come for Missy like that? I looked up at the ceiling as if Tommy could hear my thoughts.

My experiences with men bubbled over and I probably unintentionally took it all out on him. I had enough from the opposite sex, especially abuse. Whether it was physical or mental, it seemed to always be a part of my interaction.

I exhaled short breaths, tugging my long strings of bone straight weave trying to process it all. I pointed as if someone was sitting in front of me. "Why Tommy? Why?" I scraped vomit off my hands with my nubby nails convincing myself that I did a good deed for the sake of mankind.

Blood still leaked from several areas of my arm. An officer walked into the room not saying a word.

"Please, sir. Please, tell them to let me out of here."

I looked up at a window directly across from me pointing my middle finger and waving it back and forth. "You devils. You know this ain't right. It was self-defense!" My voice squeaked like a mouse caught in a trap. I guess that's because that's who I was at the moment. A mouse fighting to get free. Again. How many times would I let men take my power away from me? Tommy was dead, but I was here. A man had stolen my power again.

A woman walked in the room behind the officer. She gasped at the blood dripping from my arm.

"Oh my God," she hollered. She dropped her notepad. "Ms. Hanks, you're bleeding all over the place. Someone get some help."

Startled by the sudden call for support, I swung my arm around creating bigger droplets.

I yelled, "Yes, I'm bleeding. Tell me something I don't know lady. And you are?"

"I'm Detective Barnes. You need to get cleaned up."

With a sophisticated, southern tone, I said, "I will be just fine, thank you."

"Ms. Hanks, do you know why you are here?"

Puzzled by her line of questioning I responded, "Of course. Don't talk to me like I'm stupid. Where is my lawyer, lady? Write this down and tell the people up top." I gazed at the window again, "It was self- defense now let me go home. Why hasn't my attorney gotten here yet?"

"We want to help you, Ms. Hanks."

"I don't need your help. No matter what this looks like, I am free in Jesus name."

"Free? What makes you feel free after stabbing a man eighteen times?"

"Because I am released from all the lies, all the judgment, and all the hurt. God allowed me to find a way to dump all of my troubles." I concealed my tears as I adjusted the elastic around my waist that fit tightly around my abdomen.

Ms. Barnes responded as if she were insulted, "God? I don't think God would have wanted you to be free by killing someone, Ms. Hanks."

"Who asked you what God thinks?"

Ms. Barnes looked at the officer with disbelief.

"Ms. Hanks, I think we need to get you some serious help. If you think what you did was normal, we need you to talk to someone about this."

"God is my help and I have already talked to him today. Now get my lawyer." I tilted my head back as if I was sitting under a scalding hot shower enjoying the steam hitting my face. The more they glared, the more I leaned back with my arms reaching backward.

Voices from the officer's walkie-talkie were heard as he dispatched for help. The response back made his eyes dart in my direction. He stepped closer and whispered, "Ms. Hanks, you have a visitor."

"Well, it's about time my attorney got here." I knew Natalia would take care of me.

I killed a man. What should I say?

The truth in this instance was not going to set me free. I needed justice to prevail with a touch of God's grace and mercy. I put my head down.

I needed some form of relief.

TEN

MICHELLE

¹A tall, thin light-skinned woman with long stringy hair entered the room. She pushed her hair back as my eyes followed her every move.

She can't be the attorney with shoes that high. Is she a reporter? No can't be. They wouldn't let a reporter in the interrogation room.

Her perfume lingered. A fake fur coat wrapped around her body with portions of it swinging onto her shoulders. She shuffled her feet a bit due to her six-inch red bottom heels, but she pressed on anyway with a slight bounce like a boss.

Her hands pressed loosely on her chin. "Well, hello lady. Good to see you."

She surveyed the room sitting down on the edge of her seat making herself comfortable before I could give a response. My questioning expression remained while the woman opened her mouth, exposing her dark brown gums with two missing teeth.

"I'm sorry, but I don't think we know each other. Do we? Are you representing me?"

"Something like that. We haven't officially met in person. But I'm sure you've heard of me."

I turned my head sideways trying to understand who she was and why she was here.

"My name is Olivia Wallace...Missy's biological mother. It's such a pleasure to finally meet one of her friends."

My eyes crossed as if Olivia carried a deadly disease.

"Say what?" You are joking, right? How in the world did you get in here?" I sneered.

Her smile remained while her tongue flapped between the open space on her top gum. "All of that doesn't matter. I came to put a little bug in your ear, Michelle. Since you are the showstopper on my high definition video, I want to give you a proposition. Let's make a deal, shall we?"

It was obvious this deal wasn't going to be like the game show with the opportunity of choosing from three closed doors and Wayne Brady as the host.

"How dare you show up here." I barked.

She gave a facetious chuckle.

"How do you know my name?"

"It doesn't take a rocket scientist to figure out who you are, homegirl. You're all over the news. I know all about you."

I put my hand on my elbows, bewildered by her boldness.

"I'll keep this short because I know they got cameras in here." She tapped long acrylic blue nails onto the glass. Her nose twitched like the wicked witch of the South in a Judy Garland movie.

"What kind of deal can you give me, lady?"

She whispered. "Help me get all my money from Henry Jones and I'll keep this video of you slashing that man up to myself."

"Money? How does he owe you money? From my understanding, you abandoned your child. If anything, you owe him money."

She pulled out a cigarette flickering a yellow lighter. "I have a clear video of you doing your dirt. I'm sure the prosecuting attorney would love to have it to support locking you up for life. The tobacco stick fizzled. She put it up to her mouth and inhaled the smoke.

"Get out of here with that nonsense, lady. It was self-defense. Your video can't do anything to me."

"Oh, yes it will! Somebody told you to stop stabbing that boy in the video, and you kept going. That's not self-defense in the eyes of the law. It's stone cold murder."

My lips thinned. "That video doesn't carry any weight. The

judge will throw that mess out of court in a heartbeat. I guess *Law and Order* aren't one of your shows, huh?" I was amused at her unpolished plot.

She waved her hand. "Please don't kid yourself. Once they see this video, honey you'll be shipped to the women's prison in Raleigh faster than you can say your full name."

She winked, tilting the cigarette upward.

"Whatever. I can't help you lady and you are wasting my time."

I remembered Missy shouting in the pastor' study. "Olivia wanted her money and had a video of the murder."

Out of curiosity, I asked, "How does he owe you money?

How much?"

"One hundred thousand big ones. I even have the agreement in writing."

"Stop lying, lady."

She pulled out a tarnished piece of stationery with brown edges. She shoved it over to my side of the table. I read silently.

I Henry Jones will pay Olivia Wallace one hundred thousand dollars along with the deed to Mt. Zion Holiness Church if I am the pastor at the time of payment. It is with the intent that Olivia Wallace will leave Missy

Rochelle Jones in Durham, NC with me and my future wife Sylvia Wallace who will act as her biological mother. I will raise her to be a powerful woman of God to continue the Jones family legacy.

Pastor Jones' signature was in cursive below the first statement. A second paragraph stated the following:

✦I Olivia Wallace agree to the terms and conditions of this letter. I will remain absent from Missy's life until her twenty-seventh birthday. This will give her time to mature and finish college as requested. I agree to love her from afar and allow Minister Henry Jones to raise her while giving her the principals needed to lead the church. Please give her all the love and tender care she needs in my absence. My niece Sylvia will act as her permanent caregiver and rear her into a beautiful and respected woman of God that the Jones family desires.

P.S. Please let Missy know her mother loves her and that she will be missed.

Olivia's signature was imprinted at the bottom half of the notice.

My tone heightened. "Um Lady, this sounds like a personal problem. You and Pastor Jones need to have a 'come to Jesus' meeting. Y'all need to work this out without involving me."

"Nah, baby cakes. I just made it your problem now. If you don't help me get my money, this video will be a YouTube classic, national worldwide news, a written bestselling novel, and distributed to every alpha male in the state of North Carolina. Oh, and let's not forget all the pro-black organizations that get tired of sorry women like you killing them off."

My torso rose up. I wanted to reach over and slap a few more of her teeth out of her mouth.

"You have the audacity to come here with insults and then think that I'm going to help you? Do you know who you're dealing with? The Jones family won't lay down easily for a con artist like you. *Believe that.*" Unfazed, Olivia rubbed her chin and brushed across her facial hair. "Call it what you want, baby girl. I'm not conning anyone. That's his handwriting clear as day."

I shook my finger. "You will never get away with this."

"Watch me. I have so much dirt on you, I can make that little apple head of yours spin for days." She smiled widely licking her lips. Olivia flicked her cigarette to the floor and laughed.

"I don't see anything funny, heifer."

She reached down into her padded bra and pulled out a pink cell phone. Her shoulders bounced up and down. "Oh, you think I don't have nothin,' huh?"

I gasped as the video rolled on her high definition screen. "Oh, don't look crazy now, little church girl."

"Why are you doing this? I don't even know you."

"You the one that killed the boy. Don't blame me for being at the right place and time to see it."

I didn't have anything else to say nor was I concerned about her threats.

"All that mouth you just had. What's up now?"

"You're just an old and miserable neighborhood ghetto bunny with missing front teeth. I can't believe Pastor Jones laid down with such trash. It's time for you to leave with all this nonsense."

"Well, word on the street is that you've been laying down with some folks yourself. So, who is really the trash around here?"

I slammed my hand down, yelling and pointing towards the cameras for help. "Can someone come in and escort this lady out. She is false representing my attorney."

Olivia wiped her forehead clean pulling out another cigarette still holding onto the phone.

My scream was heard from an officer walking past the door. "How can I help you. ladies?" The officer asked walking in slowly.

I used my southern *Becky* voice. "Please escort this lady out, she is not the attorney I was looking for."

The guard shook his head, "Alright lady... time to go."

"No problem, mista,' I was leaving anyway."

She stood up, twisting her hips to shake the wrinkles out of her dress. She took two steps and struck a pose moving her hands down her vivacious thighs to accentuate the curves.

I watched her walk away with disgust. She blew a kiss, holding her hand close to her puckered lips like Marilyn Monroe. Within seconds, she disappeared.

"Now that's a true buffoon if I ever saw one. Who is bold enough to falsify their credentials?"

The police snickered and said, "We get so busy around here. Stuff happens."

I glanced at the seat she sat in. The note with the brown edges was left behind still laying right in front of me. I grabbed it before the officer took notice pushing it down into my pocket.

ELEVEN

NATALIA

Sunday afternoon...

I had gotten word that after Michelle's interrogation, she was officially taken into custody. After hours of back and forth, the police saw fit to arrest her. I don't know what she said to them to find a probable cause but I was now fearful for her future. I hoped she didn't make any crazy statements even under pressure. I was anxiously awaiting to see her face to find out what happened?

I didn't want to make a visit to the county jail alone, but everyone else had obligations. Missy was still recovering with Beanie staying by her side and after his release from the hospital, Pastor Jones officiated sister Mary's wedding at the church. I winced at the one hundred and nineteen million dollar newly built facility entering from the Mangum Street entrance with the bright sun beaming into my eyes. A brand new courthouse and jail less than a few years old were part of the cities gentrification process. The old Main Street location was torn down last year. The open space that was left became a major business complex creating more room for local entrepreneurship.

The building was one of the tallest in the area positioned across from the Durham Bulls baseball field along with a few diverse restaurants. The latest trend in the area was beer breweries. Multiple buildings gave into the new age craving. It didn't take long for me to make it to the visitation area. I admired the south-faced windows that allowed natural light to seep in while waiting. I had been in several jails and prisons with my group whenever I had time off from work. This one didn't smell as bad as the old building on Main Street. I examined the two workers behind the desk stuffing their face with cream filled Oreos. They didn't seem at all moved about anything around them while chomping on half the package. It seemed like it was taking them forever to call me in so I could see her.

I hoped to carry on a conversation without staring at her or making her feel uncomfortable. Seeing her in an orange jumpsuit was not going to be easy. None of this was going to be easy. I didn't understand why she stabbed him eighteen times. I didn't understand it last night and even in the light of day, I still didn't get it. I didn't want to judge or make her feel even worse, but I was still shocked that her petite frame could cause so much damage.

Lord, please hold back my judgmental attitude. I wish I had some praying power right now.

Gearing myself up for her entrance, I moved my lips around practicing on presenting positive facial expressions and warm smiles. We were sisters and I wanted her to go back to her cell realizing that I was there for her no matter what. Cases like this are what I lived for. Once I became a bonified advocate, I never looked back. I supported, wrote letters, marched, and had talk sessions for times just like this. Maybe God was allowing me to get a little practice so that when this day came, I could handle the situation easily.

The noise level in the waiting room was above normal. Laughter and loud chatter permeated my ears. A door located in the back of the room opened with a guard calling my name. "Natalia Freemon. Come on back."

I entered a room full of glass with Michelle moving slowly looking discombobulated on the other side. Her mangled and untamed weave bunched up on each side of her shoulders as she used her blistered hands like a rake comb, pulling her hair down. She picked up the phone, nodding her head.

I picked up the phone and said, "I am so happy to see you!

How are you, hon?"

She gave me the look of so glad to see you too, but you better get me out of here as her eyes watered.

"I'm making it. I trust and believe in God, sis. I will be home tomorrow. I know they will let me go." She set her bruised arms on the counter, rubbing her hands together. I tried hard not to stare at them.

"I hope so too. Did you say something that triggered an arrest?"

"I was tired. I couldn't stop throwing up and I just wanted it to end. I told them what they wanted to hear, I guess. I don't know what I said."

"Sis, I had everything in place. You could have gone home last night if you would have kept your mouth shut."

She glared. "Do you know how it feels to be in a hot interrogation room for hours? Don't tell me what I should have done."

"I apologize. You are right. I have no idea."

"Well, it's too late now. I will take whatever they have to give me."

"But why if you don't have to? You're better than this?"

"Not in the eyes of man. I have so much going on. I just can't keep suffering like this. Maybe sometime in jail will help me disconnect from it all."

I eyeballed her scars. "Sitting up in here for a crime that you couldn't stop is ridiculous."

She whaled, "I deserve to be here. Trust me on this one."

"Well, I never killed anyone before, so I don't know how it affects your mindset. I just think you need some sleep."

"I'll be fine," She whispered in the handset.

"I wish I could believe you right now sis. I will be back in the morning at the arraignment. I pray that by then you will have the strength to speak and let your attorney know that this was purely self- defense. You can't stay here Sis. You just can't."

She put her hands on the glass as I raised mine. "Thank you for trying to help me Natalia. I'm glad you are my friend."

† I tried not to show emotion. I was so disappointed on where this was going for her. She didn't deserve to carry all of this on her shoulders, she didn't deserve jail time, and she didn't deserve to be sleeping somewhere else other than her own bed.

"I will do my best to fight for you, Michelle. I will be there every step of the way." It was time to end our visit. I could no longer sit and listen. I could no longer carry on with a fake smile. I was deeply saddened. What she didn't realize was she just played a major part in possibly destroying her own life. I could really use a dose of Missy's holy water right about now. I don't know what she said during that interrogation but something wasn't right.

TWELVE

MICHELLE

Arraignment...

The courthouse was filled with several individuals waiting to hear their fate. Missy, Natalia, Beanie, Pastor Jones, and Mother Smithfield sat on the front row. The honorable Judge George Miller was expected to walk in at any minute.

With the latest wooden benches, freshly painted drystone, unconventional tables, high-definition cameras, and cushioned chairs along each side of the walls, the atmosphere was more relaxing than being in a dingy cell.

I sat directly across from the jury section in silence watching people come through the double wooden doors as several offenders proceeded to enter finding a seat. It was not quite 9 o'clock, which gave the attorneys a few extra minutes to convene with clients.

ﬀThey scrambled around, trying to prepare for their cases. The attorney referred by Natalia came to my cell last night to discuss the facts. Eric Smith was his name. He was a young, tall Caucasian man with a gray suit and stringy hair rushing into the courtroom barely holding onto his briefcase with his loosened tie.

He asked the guard beside me, "May I conference with her, please? I am her appointed attorney."

The guard nodded moving over.

"Ms. Hanks? How are you feeling today?" I rolled my eyes. "You're late."

He slicked his hair back with the palm of his hand and said reluctantly, "Yes ma'am, I am. But I wanted to make sure I had all your information this morning. I've been up since 5:00 a.m. reviewing all of the documents." He winked with unwavering confidence as I huffed with very little faith.

"The Court will go over why you were arrested and possibly set a bond."

I nodded. "Can I go home?"

"Perhaps." He smiled pushing his hair back again. "Not to worry, you're in good hands with me. I get these kinds of cases all the time."

Lord, I am going to jail for the rest of my life with his help. He is looking so unstable today.

"Can I trust you?"

He smiled again. "Why, of course. Helping you to gain your freedom back is what I am here for."

I scrutinized his wrinkled suit that needed the hem to be taken out of his high rising pants. His shirt looked dingy and his shoes were plastic leather. I looked him up and down trying to understand why he continued to slick his hair back pulling it behind his ears.

"All rise." The bailiff shouted. Everyone stood up at attention awaiting the judge to step up to the bench. He accelerated up the steps leering down at the audience.

"Good morning, everyone. Let's get started, shall we?" He nodded his head at the bailiff. "Our first case will involve Michelle Hanks. Ms. Hanks, will you please stand?" I shuffled my feet moving closer to the middle of the courtroom floor. My handcuffs were loosely fit and my uniform sagged. The judge put his head down to read the notes in front of him. "Ms. Hanks do you have legal representation at this time?"

"Yes, your Honor." My attorney stood several feet behind me directing me over to the defendant's desk.

"Good Morning, your Honor. I will be representing Ms. Hanks." Mr. Smith bellowed standing over me the closer I moved toward the desk.

"Good. So, I assume everyone is ready to get started?" He observed the prosecutor and then back at the defendant's table. The prosecuting attorney spoke with boldness, "Yes, we are ready, your Honor."

ᵧMy attorney fired back. "We're also ready, your Honor."

The judge spoke with a southern drawl. "I have reviewed the evidence presented by both parties." He looked over at the prosecutor again. "Is there any other information that either party would like to present?"

The prosecutor answered, "Yes, your Honor. We the state of North Carolina would like to enter seven more documents for your review. May we approach the bench?"

"Why certainly."

The prosecutor spoke out to the entire court moving towards the bench wearing a black crisp designer suit with a silk tie with gold tipped shoes.

"Your Honor, after reviewing some of the evidence captured by the investigation team, it has been determined that Ms. Michelle Hanks stabbed Mr. Tommy Lee Davis eighteen times with a nine-inch blade. Evidence shows that even after being told on several occasions to stop stabbing him by her peers, she continued to ram the knife into his side repeatedly."

"Alright. Continue." The judge said.

"We the state of North Carolina feel that the evidence given is linked to the previous relationship that Mr. Davis and Ms. Hanks shared. We have enough evidence to consider second degree murder against the defendant."

I looked back to see their faces. Natalia and Missy sat behind me with dropped mouths. The crowd wheezed at the prosecutor's statement. "Alright," The judge responded, rubbing his chin.

"I disagree. Ms. Hanks was under attack and was forced to protect herself that evening in the pastor's study. I don't know what past relationship that the prosecutor is speaking of. They had been friends for years and Ms. Hanks along with other witnesses have stated the nature of their friendship all throughout the evidence as only being very good friends," Mr. Smith said.

"Alright," The judge mumbled into the microphone.

The prosecutor handed over a stack of papers to the judge. *Murder?* I stood up trying desperately not to show any emotion. *I wanted Tommy alive just as much as Missy did.*

"Ms. Hanks, do you realize the charges that will presumably be filed against you?"

"Yes, your Honor, but I'm not a killer. I was only trying to defend myself." I dropped my hands in front of me as my handcuffs clinked.

"Alright... Defense, do you have any documents to add?"

"Your Honor, Ms. Hanks is far from being a cold-blooded killer. The man came in armed and dangerous. She had to defend herself and others around her due to such a perilous situation. I did not find anything in the evidence presented that proves a probable cause for murder. And with that being said, I have no other documents to present."

"Well, based upon the plethora of evidence I now hold in my hands. I will set a bail amount." He looked down again pulling off his reading glasses. "The bail is set for five hundred thousand dollars."

⸱ Mr. Smith bent down and whispered in my ear, "Not to worry, Ms. Hanks. This is a no-brainer, we will win this."

I didn't flinch as I used the judge's full head of gray hair as my focal point and stared straight ahead. He threw down his gavel and shouted, "Next case."

Mr. Smith followed me out of the courtroom with a guard on the other side. "Ms. Hanks, I want to be honest with you. At the end of the day, you murdered someone. This won't be easy but I will make sure you get out of here. But I must ask Ms. Hanks. Did you have a deeper relationship more than a friendship with Mr. Davis? Did you sleep with the deceased? Did you have something going on with Tommy Lee Davis?"

I didn't answer as I ogled the steel doors ahead of me.

"Knowing the A.D.A, he will do everything possible to stick with a murder charge but my goal is to continue to reiterate self-defense and why. That's how he operates. I've been down this road with him many times before."

"Could this possibly be jail time Mr. Smith if they don't believe me?" I asked as our feet banged against the floor only a few more inches away from the jail entrance.

"Perhaps. North Carolina laws can be complicated. There are some cases that require jail time while others might allow probation. So many variables to consider. All I can say is we have a long road ahead of us on this one if we're taking it to trial. But I know what I'm doing, so don't worry."

Tommy was my friend. I never meant to kill him.

"I'm not sure I want to go through a trial, Mr. Smith."

He shook his head and said, "Well sleep on it and we will go over your options again. See you in a few days, Ms. Hanks. It is a pleasure to work with you."

I tilted my head to the side only with a smidgen of dignity left. The guard shifted to the other side swinging the door back quietly. I didn't know how I was going to get someone to bail me out. But until someone came to rescue me, I had to return to block five, cell twenty-two.

THIRTEEN

MISSY

I called a meeting of the board. Daddy was determined to get Michelle out of jail and wanted to discuss it with the decision makers of the church. I sat at the head of the oval-shaped table in the conference room. I tried to make sense of Michelle's case and the cruel things that the prosecution said to win over the judge.

The board members filed in and moved around the table to their designated seats. Light conversation about the case was held as we waited for Sister Mary to arrive. She was in charge of the minutes for each meeting and we couldn't start without her.

Sister Mary rushed in wearing a floral jacket with a matching scarf and slid into her seat. "Alright we ready?" she said breathing hard.

Daddy rolled his eyes looking peeved at her tardiness. "We have been ready for a while now gal. The question is...are you ready?"

She cleared her throat and grabbed a pen placing her notebook on the table landing her eyes on only what was directly in front of her.

Daddy started the meeting moving his hands up and down to express his concern.

"Thank you for coming on such a short notice. We're here today to discuss Michelle Hanks and her status with her trial. Her hearing today at the county courthouse was not believed to be in her favor. A bond of five hundred thousand dollars was set. Can you believe that? I don't want her mother to have to handle all the burden and responsibility of bailing her out."

"Hum," Mother Smithfield mumbled.

Daddy rolled his eyes. "Anyway, Michelle is a third generation Mt. Zion member and we should do whatever we can to help her out with this situation. Amen?"

"Amen," The board repeated, except Mother Smithfield.

"Since when we start bailing folks out of jail?" Mother Smithfield asked.

"Just hear me out."

She shook her head. "Go ahead."

"Now, we have a large amount of residual income in our

fundraiser and mission account. We haven't had to use it because the community hasn't reached out to us that much this year for assistance. Ain't God good? So, the Deacon and I will go this afternoon to make a withdrawal to get her out of that hell hole. All transactions should be finalized no later than tomorrow evening."

"What I want to know is what made her stab the boy like that to get her in all this mess in the first place? She is deemed a murderer right now, right?" Mother Smithfield asked.

"Mother, our concern is protecting our own when we know they deserve better treatment. We can't rehash the crime. We need to focus on helping her."

She flung her hands in the air to express that she didn't care. "Well, I am not about to agree with helping a killer. Whether she is a church member or not, she killed a man."

"Don't let the devil use you, mother. If we don't do something to help, she could sit in there until this case is over. That could take years if we don't take action."

Mother Smithfield settled down and sat attentively.

"Lord knows that is the truth. My cousin Bunky sat in the county jail for almost two years straight. He was innocent and shouldn't been waiting that long with all that evidence they had on the actual shooter. They move so slow downtown and don't seem to care about our people," Mother Agnes said.

"I know that's right. This type of stuff goes on all the time." Mother Gaines replied.

"Well, it's not about to happen on our watch. Michelle's bravery is the reason why Missy and I are sitting here at this table today. If she didn't come to our rescue and take that man down, we would not be living to tell about it."

Mother Gaines lifted her hand to speak. "Passuh, so what are we gonna do about all this news coverage on the church property? The media is blowing this way out of proportion and they are making us look bad. Even that woman's domestic violence group is going national with this story. I heard some folks say they ain't stepping foot back in this place since we can't seem to control our monthly crime scenes. Even with all that security that you are paying top dollar for, folks just don't feel safe anymore."

"God did not give us a spirit of fear Mother Gaines so if they want to leave, let them go. I can't chain down the doors and hold folks in here every Sunday. All I can do is leave it all in God's unchanging hands."

"I know that's right." Sister Mary looked up for a few seconds and then back down again scribbling across her notebook paper.

"So, here's the plan, folks. As soon as we adjourn this meeting, Deacon Freemon and I will start the process."

"How much you need to take out?" Mother Smithfield asked.

"Three hundred thousand dollars?"

"What? Passuh, that doesn't even sound right. Why so much?" She barked.

Daddy gave her a stern look of don't question me written all over his face. He then cleared his throat and said, "Excuse me, I meant two hundred thousand."

Sister Mary took out a red pen out of her purse to underline the last portion of her notes as Mother Smithfield looked back with a contentious stare.

Two hundred thousand?

"Will this money be replenished sooner than later. Passuh? What if she is found guilty?" Mother Smithfield said rattling her cane and examining daddy's uneased disposition.

"Trust me, there is no way on God's green earth she is going down for protecting folk. And of course, it will be replenished. When she wins the case, it will all be paid back to us in full."

"Dag nab it, does anyone care that a man's life was taken by this woman? Let the chips fall where they should on this one, Passuh."

"I will not," Daddy replied.

"Are we reaching out to Tommy's family to give them money? What makes Michelle so dog on special?" Her cane bounced on the linoleum floor as she squirmed in her seat looking displeased. If looks could kill, we would have all dropped dead as she scanned the room threatening us with her eyes. She contorted her smirk into a frown of hatred.

"Do you realize how much that girl has done for this church?" Daddy pulled his handkerchief out blowing his nose.

Looks were exchanged without a response.

"Well, I do feel sorry for that boy and his family. You got a point there. But, what I want to know is, what are we going to do about a musician? Even after being released, Michelle still won't be able to play for the church until this all boils over. It's so much scrutiny surrounding this and I think it's best she be sat down for a while." Deacon Freemon said pushing his suspenders out and snapping them back on his chest.

"You are right about that." Sister Mary responded batting her eyes back at him. Daddy hated it when she couldn't self-contain her feelings. He was quick to put her in check each time she showed any form of eye seduction. Everyone knew she was madly in love with James Freemon. She wasn't the only one. He was the church ladies' popular choice to flirt with. He carried himself around like an old retired pimp and was still a womanizer long after his wife's death.

"I think Daryl is doing a fine job filling in for Michelle. I say let's vote for him to become the interim musician until further notice." Deacon Freemon said.

"I agree." I lifted my hand up as my stomach growled.

"All in favor?" Daddy shouted.

Seven responses of "Yea" rung out simultaneously. The eighth voice dropped her cane in frustration.

"Again, you are all missing the point." Mother Smithfield said.

"Any questions or concerns?" Daddy asked ignoring Mother Smithfield's lack of participation.

Mother Smithfield lifted her index finger slowly. "I think we are done here, Passuh. But I would like to speak with you in private." She motioned for everyone to leave the room by lifting her cane and pointing to the door. The board members looked around with surprised expressions on their faces. The office evacuated as mother leaned back into her chair becoming undignified.

I shut the door completely putting my ears close to it. I could hear her change her tone through the door. "Why the *hell* are you taking out that kind of money, Henry? You must think we're a bunch of idiots sitting around this table."

His eyes wandered around the room not looking at her eye to eye.

"We all know that amount ain't ten percent of her bail bond requirement. Furthermore, we ain't got no business as a church body bailing folks out of jail."

"Now mother…"

"Don't you dare now mother me. I know you better than you know yourself, Chile. I helped you as an infant while you were fighting that horrible blood disease, changed your stinking cloth diapers, and fed you meals every time your mother had to work in them factories to make ends meet."

"I know mother."

"And this is how you honor her legacy? By lying to board members about what you about to do with the church's money? What has gotten into you, Henry?"

I peeked through the crack in the door wanting to see his facial expression.

Daddy sighed. He began to rub his forearm in the way he always did when he was nervous or uncertain.

"Nothing for you to worry about mother."

"I smell a rat up in here! I hate to call my pastor of fifteen years a liar but Lord knows, you trying to pull a fast one on these members. What you got up your sleeve now Henry?"

Daddy rolled his eyes.

"After taking out a second and third mortgage on this building, no one should trust you with a dime."

What???

"Are you planning to pay off Olivia? I know Michelle's family is loaded with money to bail her out. They don't need us."

"You don't know that mother."

"Yes, I do. The farming life got them set for life financially."

"Mother please…"

"Olivia made the kitchen too hot for you, huh? So now you want to pay her off and run from your responsibilities once again?" She shook her finger in the air. "I tell you right now if you start a dogfight with that crazy woman, you gonna have to finish it!"

Daddy plopped his hands down on the table. "Mother Smithfield, please let me handle my own personal affairs for once. It was my sweat that got the funds to accumulate in that account. Ain't the money for the community?"

She hissed.

"Well, that's what we are doing, supporting someone in need from the community mother."

"You got these folks believing we saving a murderer, but yet we saving you? That is what this is really about…isn't it, Henry?"

"Every time I make a move you know about it and want to give your personal opinions on it. I am tired of explaining myself to you. You are just the mother of the church, not the finance officer."

She sputtered back, "You better watch your tone with me

Passuh before I put you over my knee like you were two again. Shame on you and your trifling self. At the end of the day, not one dime of that money belongs in your personal pocket."

"I run this ship."

"And so far, it's sinking."

"Who asked you, Mother?"

She balled up her fist and said, "My only job in this church has been to protect you. I promised your mother and I'm not going back on my word because you're too darn silly to see your wrongdoing. If the members find out about all your money shuffling foolishness along with the rest of your dirt, you gonna lose this here church for good. I hope the IRS swoops down and show you something."

"I'm doing this for Missy. Everything I do, I do to help her and this church."

Mother's cane hit the floor as she kicked her leg up in rage. "You doing it for yourself. I rebuke that lying demon! Stop feeding that girl more lies. You know you made her the HNIC (Head Negro in Charge) so that Olivia couldn't get everything she asked for in that original agreement. It's time to come clean, Henry."

"Hush Mother."

"That gal's anointing is the only reason this church stays packed Sunday after Sunday. She's also the reason why all those mortgages are getting paid."

"Mother..." He slammed his fist down on the table.

"I refuse to keep quiet Henry. One day I am going to tell it all."

"Mother Smithfield, you gonna stop trying to turn my daughter against me you hear? Hush now. You talking way too much."

"Henry, don't keep doing that girl like this. I am telling you. In the end, it's gonna come back and bite you right in the middle of your behind."

"Thanks for the advice, but I will be calling Olivia sometime today so she can come and get her money."

She blew her breath rubbing up against the table as it held her sagging boobs up. "Shame before God, Henry."

"Call it what you want to call it, Mother. I'm gonna pay her. End of story."

Daddy had nothing else to say as I continued to squint my eyes through the crack of the door. It was his last word and final benediction over the matter. I jumped back from the door and sat in the seat in the hallway with my legs crossed, wishing I hadn't heard any of that conversation.

I knew I couldn't confront him today about all of this for sure. It was hard to talk to him about church business. But I had to stand my ground and learn how to one day; now being the acting pastor and leader of the congregation. He rubbed his hands together walking past me and into the sanctuary.

Mother Smithfield eased out of her seat, walking behind him. She stood in front of me and said, "I want to encourage your dear heart to keep getting better with Christ. You're the saving grace of this ministry."

I didn't know what to say but I needed to give her some form of a hint that I knew what I was dealing with. "I know Mother... God takes care of babies and fools."

She grabbed my hand and winked. "He shole do, Passuh... he shole do."

• All I could think about was why in the world does a saved man keep so many secrets and lies locked away from his only living heir? How can he possibly have my best interest at heart with all this chaos going on in the church? And most of all I thought, when will he realize that this isn't part of Gods plan for our family name? No preacher should act like this.

Once again, I felt embarrassed, hurt, and betrayed. I was going to have to clean up behind his foolishness again. But this time was going to be the last time. I was not going to allow my daddy to disrupt the house of God, again. It should be about souls, not about lies and deception.

I put my head down in shame. God, please guide me every step of the way to fix this mess. What would the church say if I kicked my own daddy off the board? He had to go… no doubt about that.

FOURTEEN

MISSY

My job wasn't to raise my daddy. My grandmother did that already. He was stuck in his ways and had unwavering beliefs on how to handle certain things. He thought money solved every problem within the universe, not realizing that the love of money is the root of all evil.

My only assignment was to keep a leveled head for the sake of God's people and preach the gospel. Daddy was about to mess everything up for the church and my days of not taking full responsibility for the Jones family legacy were over. Bringing souls to Christ was now my priority. Saving the family name was second.

It had been thirteen whole days since Tommy died. It had

also been thirteen whole days that Michelle was identified as his killer. The coroner kept his body for over a week. Everything dragged, it seemed to almost take as long to get Michelle out of jail. Her mother bailed her out. Who knows what daddy did with the church money.

Michelle wanted to attend the funeral. I knew allowing her to do so would bring discomfort to some of Tommy's friends, family and even me. I didn't want her around me but I tried desperately to feel some form of compassion for her. I would only allow her to watch the funeral from the balcony. That was her best bet.

We all agreed to meet in the corridor of the church thirty minutes before the funeral started. Michelle came inside the church incognito wearing a wig, glasses, and a big oversized hat that stretched down over her face. The others were dressed in black from head to toe.

This was going to be a tough goodbye. I immediately asked everyone to say a word of prayer before going into the sanctuary. We curved around one another holding hands and bowing our heads.

Daddy moved his hands around and said a few sentences ending it with, "In Jesus precious name we pray, Amen."

"Amen."

"Be strong Missy," Natalia said walking alongside Beanie and

Michelle.

"I will do my best."

"I'm so sorry Missy." Michelle sniveled breaking away from the others and moving quickly up the balcony stairs. She looked as if she had been up all night crying as her eyes sagged way below her sunglasses. She pushed the gold frame high up on her face without looking back. I guess she wasn't expecting a response from me. That was very wise on her part because I had no intentions to look at her more less speak to her.

I followed Daddy into the study in need of some father-daughter time. I wanted to address what I heard after the board meeting. Another prayer wouldn't hurt either as I desired some consultation. I plopped down in the recliner watching him pull a big black-and-white starched robe off the door hook, removing the plastic and sliding it over his clothes. It had been cleaned and starched for the occasion.

The funeral was scheduled for 1 o'clock while the viewing of the body started at noon. I viewed the television monitor in the corner of the office noticing hundreds of people proceeding in slowly. Daddy glanced over as he reached inside the mini refrigerator next to the door pursing his lips up and downing another can of diet coca cola.

"So, what did you and Mother Smithfield talk about after the board meeting?"

"Nothing important."

I crossed my hands in my lap. "I beg to differ."

He didn't look up. He rubbed his forearm. I guess our father- daughter time wasn't going as he planned.

"What is it, gal? I thought you would be in here falling out and tears dropping on the carpet. But instead, you questioning me? Say what you got to say."

"You've been embezzling church funds and think you're going to get away with it? Are you serious?"

"Look gal. I am under a lot of stress. Let it go."

I closed my eyes gaining the strength to formulate my words. "Daddy, do you realize you are a hypocrite?"

It was as if smoke came out of his nostrils. "What did you say to me, gal?"

"You are a hypocrite. There I said it. Until you get it right with God, you will always be stressed."

His eyes stretched. "You better watch your tone. I got a mind to backhand you right where you stand."

"Why because I am calling it how I see it? You know what your problem is daddy? You never wanted to be in ministry in the first place. You only did it to please grandma. You loved being out there in the streets. That's how you met up with Olivia. You have played the role of a preacher but deep down inside, this is not what you want."

93

"I'm gonna need you to hush your mouth gal. This is not the place or the time for this kind of talk. Let's lay this boy to rest and I will handle you and your smart mouth later." He started breathing hard with sorrowful eyes. *I used to respect him to the utmost until now.*

I crossed my legs and raised a finger to massage my throbbing temple. "There won't be a later daddy. After we finish putting this man in the ground, I will be calling all the board members to consider removing you from the board."

"You will do no such thing." He shouted.

"It's time daddy. If I don't, when we get audited, someone is going to do time for your mistakes."

Standing tall and lean with a clean-cut beard, daddy checked himself again before leaving out. He ignored my demand and grabbed my hand. "Lord, I'm asking you, help us through such a time as this. Give Missy the courage and strength she needs for this service. Lord, I am asking that you heal her body completely of any anxiety, attacks, or speech problems. Let her mind come back as she is losing it slowly. It's in Jesus' name we pray."

I snatched my hand from his. "Say what you want. You will be voted off and I need you to give all the money back that you have stolen over the years."

"All of it?"

"Every penny."

♪"Where am I going to get that kind of money from gal? What you gonna do, turn me in or something?"

I folded my arms. "If I have too. That is what real Christians do. They do the right thing in the eyes of God. You know anything about that, Daddy?"

He nodded looking away. He knew I meant business. "Well, you are the pastor now. I am not going to go against you daughter. I will respect your office of authority. I just hope I get it right with God before I leave this here earth."

"Good." I finally spoke up for me, my family, and the church without buckling. *I know grandma is in heaven proud.*

He waited for me to go through the office doors first as he ran his fingers through his beard again moving sideways to adjust his white shirt underneath his robe. He reached down to the hem of his garment to ensure it was dust free. It was time to enter the sanctuary as the purple clock above the bookshelf displayed 12:58 pm. We held onto one another gearing up to walk in with dignity. We were arm in arm just like I envisioned for my wedding with Tommy. But instead of saying "I do", I was probably going to walk down the aisle saying, "Please, don't leave me."

"Such an unfair way of leaving this earth, I declare." He turned and looked at me as If he could read my thoughts and whispered in my ear. "Now listen daughter, don't you go in there falling out and stuff. Keep yourself together, gal. You know WRAL and all the smartphones in town are going to be on you. Also, remember the promise you made to Beanie."

It only took a matter of minutes to get my daddy back. The caring, loving, and sweet man that always had my back and supported me was present. I knew he was going to have to sit somewhere and allow my words to marinate in his brain. He knew I spoke the truth and I think he was somewhat relieved as his breathing went back to normal. I'm sure he was probably glad that he didn't have to hide things from me anymore.

———

Women of all colors, shapes, and sizes waltzed in putting their hands over their mouths in disbelief. Tommy laid peacefully. Soft music playing in the background. Daddy shook his head and said, "I sure wish I could be somewhere else at the moment. This is going to be a rough one daughter."

We marched down from the back of the church as daddy nodded his head with a what's up to several individuals.

I glimpsed at the entire congregation recognizing some of the faces. Tommy had several cuddle buddies that I confronted over the years sitting in the first three rows. Beanie sat in the front with Natalia next to some of Tommy's family looking back at me.

Michelle was settled in the balcony with cameras scrolling up top displaying her holding her head low and looking down at the floor. She pulled her large hat off while tilting to the side of the pew. With her Peggy Bundy wig on, she didn't have to worry about being recognized.

Tommy was dressed in a white suit with a red handkerchief and matching tie. His hands were crossed holding a white mini Bible that rested on his midsection. His hair was slicked back and a diamond earring hung from his right ear. Holloway Funeral Home made him look just like he did when he was alive. He appeared to be sleeping. I know well how he looked when he slept. I knew well how his handsome dimples continued to tease me even when he was deep in his sleep.

I tried to hold back my tears as we continued to move closer to the casket. We reached my designated chair as daddy lifted my arm helping me up the steps of the pulpit. He bent down kissing me on my forehead and then moved to the podium. He was the designated master of ceremony. He started the service with a praise.

"Let the church say amen. Let the church say amen again."

"Amen."

"Oh, come on, come on, come on. Down in these parts, we

don't call this occasion a funeral. We call it a home going service. Amen?"

"Amen." The church responded with several screams and claps to follow.

"Oh, we are not about to be sad today. Uh-uh, God now has a musical angel in heaven! Amen?"

"Amen." The Church reeled back standing on their feet and clapping with celebratory cheers.

The ushers passed around color filled programs as daddy seemed to work hard to get everyone to loosen the spirit of mourning and enter the service with true praise.

"God is still worthy church. Do you hear what I say? God still gets all the glory and he deserves all the honor in this place. Can I get a witness somebody?"

The musical section revved up while a tall and dark heavy-set woman with braids jumped out of her seat and into the middle aisle. She was putting in work with a two-step holy dance and moving her feet from side to side. One of the mothers on the front row joined in as her white hat flapped up and down. It became a domino effect with other individuals popping up and praising God along with them.

I tuned it all out while holding a copy of the program with a tight grip ogling the photos placed throughout. Several pictures of Tommy were displayed from birth up until his college years.

He had several poses with his brother. They dressed alike for several occasions even though they had a four-year difference in age. Baby pictures of him lying on his back and smiling widely with his distinctive large dimples were posted on the back. Even as a baby, he had a smile that would make you smile back if you stared long enough. Two poems, a prayer, and words from his brother were also part of the four pages, eight by eleven program.

Once the dancing ceased, daddy lifted the microphone again. "Today we are here to celebrate the life of our brother, Tommy Lee Davis, a fine musician and a faithful member of Mt. Zion Holiness church for five years. He will be missed by so many, and I want to express my condolences to his brother and sister-in-law at this time."

His brother looked up and gave a nod.

"If we could all stand for a moment of prayer and then after that, Sister Monica will read the obituary." The congregation stood as commanded.

Darryl Boone, the fill-in musician, played "It is Well with My Soul" softly. He gave the proper signals right away with his head nodding, subtle signaling, and lots of smiling to keep daddy on track.

Natalia and Beanie observed my every move with parted lips and arms folded. I tried to sit up straight in my black-and-white silk robe holding a matching handkerchief upright as the cameras circulated.

Occasionally, I found myself leaning over as my heart felt heavy but then the camera would point in my direction making me sit up straight again. The laced handkerchief swished back and forth like a flag as my feet tapped double time on the pulpit carpet.

———

After Sister Monica sat down, the atmosphere had changed back into mourning, Daddy responded quickly. "Saints, this is not a time to feel down and out. This is a celebration of life, and we should treat it as such. Tommy had a good life. What a fine reading of the obituary. Thank you, sister Monica." She smiled switching her tiny hips in a short black suit. She bounced back to her seat while her silky bobbed hairstyle moved with her walk.

"Alright, come on choir." He signaled for Mr. Holloway, the funeral director to come up to the front. It was time to close the casket and move on with the service. The director stepped closer rubbing the side of the casket with his white gloves. His designer suit looked fresh off the rack as he straightened his jacket waiting for assistance. The other funeral home workers moved forward stopping right beside him. He folded back the black and gold overlay casket skirt while one of the assistants inched the top down slowly. The other one turned at attention and looked out into the audience preparing for any form of outbreak as the casket's top closed completely.

A young lady with bright red weave ran down the aisle jumping up and down in front of the casket's stationary bars screaming, "No, not my Tommy, Lord."

She reached over trying to put her hand on the top as the worker moved her aside gently allowing his coworkers to complete the task at hand. They moved the large spray of red and white flowers to the center of the casket and remained standing on each side until the music shifted.

Another dark-skinned sister rushed up from the back of the church running forward and stretching her hands in front of her body screaming, "Why Lord? Why?"

Daddy didn't seem at all surprised as he pressed his lips onto the microphone ignoring the behavior. "Come on choir. Give us that selection please."

The choir stood up in unison as the two women bent over walking back to their seats. Tambourines and hymn books were picked up as the choir roared loudly. They carried on as if it was a regular Sunday morning service. Pastor Jenkins, the head pastor over the Southern District stood up clapping his hands and signaling that he was soon ready to deliver the eulogy.

The choir sang the last chorus as daddy shuffled papers in front of him. He gave a brief introduction of the speaker to the congregation reading a long synopsis of Pastor Jenkins background and ended it with, "I present to some and introduce to others, Pastor Jenkins the great leader of the Southern district. Stand up and receive him as he comes to give us a powerful word from the Lord." A few hallelujahs and thank you Jesus came from the crowd as everyone stood up to honor the God in him. He grabbed the microphone from daddy and belched his words out with power and authority.

"Ah let's give God some praise up in here saints. We may endure some weeping throughout the night but joy will come in the morning." The organist moved up the musical scale as Pastor Jenkins jumped quickly into preaching formation. "To be absent from the body is to be present with the Lord, saints. We should be happy for this young man because this young soldier of ours has made it into the gates of heaven to be with the Lord. We can't say that for everyone that leaves this earth. But we can say it about Tommy Lee Davis, a true man of God. Give God some praise for this man's life," He shouted leaning sideways with the microphone. "I loved how this man found complete joy in playing that old organ. Can I get a witness?"

"Yes, Pastor, say it," Mother Gaines yelled fanning back and forth.

"See, Tommy wasn't shy. He didn't have a problem letting me know that I preached too long or my opening song was out of key." The crowd laughed at his honesty.

"Each time I visited this church or if he came to my church, he would speak his mind. But one thing was for sure, he knew God and he knew the word of God. I tell you that much. The word of God seeped deep into his heart at an early age. Amen?"

"Amen," the church fired back.

I made an eye connection with Natalia as we both rolled our eyes at the pastor's words. *Tommy may have known the word of God but the devil knows it too.* After seeing the performance from the two women, it wasn't hard to drop the sentimental look and pay attention to all the false statements made about my dead ex-boyfriend. I wiped my face and dried my eyes fast, quick, and in a hurry tapping my foot now longing for this entire charade to be over.

"Lord knows he will be missed." Pastor Jenkins picked up his Bible whispering softly into the microphone, "Turn your Bibles to Matthew five versus four and five." He began to read. "Blessed are those who mourn, for they shall be comforted." He paused to catch his breath. "Now turn to John fourteen, verses one through four." He continued to give scriptures as the congregation repeated each one after him. "The Lord said to believe in him and he will prepare a place for you. Can I get an amen?"

"Amen." The church fired back.

"See God knew what He wanted for Tommy's life before he was even born. So, I say unto you today brothers and sisters: Fear not because God will strengthen you. Don't be dismayed because God will uphold you. Hold on to God's unchanging hand and He will see you through during this time of bereavement. Can I get a witness?"

"Amen."

"For everything, there is a season. Lord have mercy. Yawl don't hear me."

"Preach Pastor," Mother Gaines shouted waving her hand in agreement.

"Let not your heart be troubled people cause' good ole Tommy is all right." He shouted with the minister's hack in his throat and dipped onto the main floor from the pulpit. "Good God from Zion. I feel like preaching in this place. See, God's got him and everything, I said everything, I said everything's gonna be alright! Good God Almighty!"

"Preach sir," a woman from the crowd yelled.

"He was a great musician and he could play any song in any key. A gifted brother. Educated. Talented. A man of God. Who could ask for anything more? He was ready to leave us because he was in good standing with the Lord. And now he is with our Father in heaven. He drew back with a hack again. "I said everything, I do mean everything is gonna be alright. Amen."

"Amen."

He yanked a towel that laid on top of the podium wiping his head and face removing all the sweat that resided. Elder Brenda Snipes was new to the usher board walked over to give him a clean one while squealing with excitement.

"Here you go, Passuh." She was happy to be near him. She put the towel on the edge of the podium, moved to the side and then looked back with a wide smile. He continued to preach without any form of acknowledgment. He was a chocolate brother and very good on the eyes. She made it known on several occasions in women's meetings and Fifth Sunday Jubilees that she desired to have him sooner than later. When she talked about him, she always looked hot and bothered as her eyes expressed, *I want him in my bedroom, now.*

"To the bereaving family, the funeral home will give you a signed Bible as a token of love from the church. Go in peace and know that Tommy is now in a better place."

Tommy's sister in law rocked her husband back and forth, rubbing his back as he leaned forward howling out in desperation. Daddy signaled for the funeral home workers to prepare for the end of the service.

"Let's give God praise in this place, church," Pastor Jenkins continued.

He bent down low bracing his knee belching out the words of *My Soul Is Anchored*. The church rocked with him as he swayed down the aisle as the pallbearers prepared for dismissal.

The billows may roll;
the breakers may dash.
My soul, my soul, my soul, my soul...

The funeral director removed the flowers off the top of the casket. Natalia and Beanie rushed up to the pulpit to comfort me. Michelle remained up in the balcony rocking. Pastor continued to sing into the microphone feeling soothed by the Holy Ghost as he got louder and louder. He sounded like T.D. Jakes with the morning gospel moment on The Light gospel radio station.

The black and white casket was raised high up in the air by eight pallbearers. Six of them being Tommy's fraternity brothers as they all wore red and white matching shirts and ties. They walked slowly with several women coming behind them carrying flowers and large plants marked *With Sympathy*.

When Pastor Jenkins sat down in his seat, the choir jumped

up again to sing the last selection as the funeral home director said, "May we all stand?"

Going Up Yonder was always the final song played at the end of every funeral at Mt. Zion.

Tommy's brother and wife filed out into the middle aisle behind the casket as the rest of the congregation followed. The burial grounds were in the backyard of the church. Over two hundred church members were laid to rest in the church's cemetery over a fifty-year time span. Tommy's body was going to be put right next to his great uncle who attended Mt. Zion a few years prior to his death. The casket was carried less than fifty feet away as the pallbearers trudged through the soft red mud and placed it over a ten-foot hole in the ground.

"Lord help us," I screamed with trickling tears.

Natalia took a double look back and said, "Get yourself together."

⸝ I pressed forward flapping my handkerchief back and forth on my side. She rubbed her fingers together and whispered again. "Cut it out I said before you have an attack out here in all this red mud. I suggest you wipe them tears, put your big girl panties on, and toughen up. You got your new man out here trying to help you thru this and folks staring down your throat. So, pull it together sis."

I used my other hand as a fan inching closer to the casket.

Her tongue-lashing seemed to work as I bent down to pick up a handful of roses from one of the flower baskets throwing them into the casket hole without tapping my foot.

While everyone filed in to hear the last and final words, Tommy's fraternity brothers gave a tribute in front of the casket as it sat high mounted above the deep hole in the ground.

"Ashes to ashes dust to dust…" Pastor Jenkins used a few words from the King James Bible of Genesis 2:7 and John 30:19 raising both arms straight into the air.

"This concludes the interment for our dear Tommy. The repast will be held in the church's dining hall area. Govern yourselves accordingly."

Balancing my elbows in the palm of my hands I continued to stand over the open space staring at the funeral home workers as they cranked the body down to the bottom of the hole.

Daddy moved beside me and said, "Wipe your face, baby girl. Beanie over there looking some kind of way. Smile and fake it for him and the cameras. WRAL just pulled up."

I looked up at the news trucks with blurred eyes as if he'd spoken in a foreign tongue. He grabbed me and turned me away from the casket shoving me into his chest. I couldn't stop my tears as I cried with my familiar snorkeling noises attempting to catch my breath. I tried to whisper so that Beanie couldn't hear us. "I'll get it together, Daddy. I just can't help it, I love him."

He hugged me tighter while muffling my breathing even more. Beanie moved in closer grabbing my hand, "You'll make it, my dear. God is your strength." I viewed his smile still resting on daddy's chest.

Daddy lifted my head with his hands placed on each side of my cheeks. "Remember all of the good times daughter—*if there were any*. Stop worrying and get your soul anchored in the Lord. I tell you that song touched me cause' only God can see us through this baby girl. It is definitely a song I needed to hear."

I looked at daddy with an incredulous gaze. He had a pastor's heart but a criminal's mind at times. I subsided my anger for him and became appreciative of the good times. Even after our chat, he still showed the love and support I needed.

I realized that I was surrounded by my own personal dream team. A solid group of individuals who I could always count on Jesus, Daddy, Beanie and Natalia as they all moved in closer for a group hug.

There was one person missing that I once considered to be part of my roster, but she wasn't anywhere around. Michelle. I looked over the huddle to see if I could catch a glimpse of her high wig and loose skirt. But she was nowhere in sight. I gazed into the parking area viewing the space she used to park her vehicle. It was empty and confirmed, Michelle had left the premises. It was a good thing. I don't know how I will ever forgive her. The Christian side of me wanted to try and make peace. But my flesh wanted her locked up for a lifetime.

FIFTEEN

MICHELLE

A month later...

I adjusted my big balloon black skirt stepping out of my truck. I was thankful for my short-lived freedom. But, I decided to give in to a plea, so the judge recommended regular attendance to a psychologist until further notice. My long thick file from childhood told the complete story on why it was necessary. I was not at all surprised that it would become a regular activity once again after killing a man.

I patted myself down wiping away perspiration before entering the big skyscraper known as Durham County Office of Mental Health. I heard several women talking at the county jail about the eye candy therapist that had women wanting a few extra visits. Dr. Do Right is what they called him. I was curious to see what all the talk was about once I heard I was assigned to Mr. Popular.

I stopped at the front desk and said, "I'm here to see Dr. Emmanuel Brown."

"Sure. State your name?"

"Michelle Hanks."

"He is waiting for you. Go right in."

I opened the door moving slowly sticking my head in from the side. "Greetings, Dr. Do Right—I mean Dr. Brown."

He crossed one lanky leg over the other, positioning a notepad upright in his lap. He adjusted his brown-rimmed glasses, looking at me up and down with a half grin.

He was definitely not the man I heard about.

He couldn't be.

He readjusted his face with a widened smile. "You must be Michelle. Sit down and make yourself comfortable." He stood up to shake my hand. "Would you like a glass of water before we get started?"

"No thank you." I moved around the office finding a seat.

His blank stare was unnerving as his crossed eyes left me confused as to what he was looking at. I stared back at him wondering *what the heck?* He was not what I pictured from the jail girl's descriptions.

"Well, you don't look like someone who's happy to be here. What's wrong, Ms. Hanks?"

"What does a killer supposed to look like, Doc?"

He reminded me of the 1980's Bill Cosby, cartoon version. To look upon the face of such a nerd with ankle boots in ninety-degree weather was disturbing.

I struggled to stay focused as he tapped his pencil on his armrest. He struggled to find questions to ask me. I couldn't get past the brown scuffed-up boots propped up on the office ottoman. His ashy ankles were exposed and screaming *lotion, please.*

I didn't have any interest in expressing how I felt about the murder. I wanted to keep it all in. It was hard to look at him eye to eye. *Does he have on Batman socks?* I observed the bottom of his legs as the yellow bat figure popped out of his boot. I tapped my nails on the table next to me impatiently, itching to get this session over with.

"So, how are you feeling now that you're out on bond?"

"Okay."

"Do you have support at home?"

I wish I could tell him about my pill addiction.

"Not really. I'm sure you read about my past. I've never had support at home. Nothing is different now that I killed someone."

Without flinching, he reached over for his I Love New York coffee mug. He sipped his coffee, making a loud slurping sound as creamed liquid splashed around his checkered shirt. He leaned forward, dropping his boot with a thump and asked, "So are you admitting to killing the man?"

Placing my hand on my chin, I responded, "Take it how you want to take it, Doc. He was going to kill us so I had to do what I had to do."

He blinked several times, looking uncomfortable. "I see."

Along with being good friends, Tommy and I had sex. He was aggressive but in a good way. I'd been secretly seeing him for years. That's all I wanted from him—that's all I needed. He was only good for fulfilling my needs. I knew I wouldn't find love. I had way too much baggage, and no man would want to deal with my past trust issues. Truth is, his sex was more addictive sometimes than my pills. I learned to disconnect the deceitful acts out of my brain just as I did my childhood and still played the role of the holy sister on the keys.

He reached over and put the coffee on the table beside him as his Batman socks stretched farther and farther outside of the length of his boots.

"Can we get this over with, please?"

He raised his eyebrows. "What's the rush, and why are you so demanding?"

"I killed him. It's over with, so what else do you want from me?" My arms shifted now feeling irritated by the small talk. "If I have to keep talking to you until my thirty minutes are up, then let's talk about medication. I need something to help me sleep."

"How many hours have you slept since the murder?"

"If I get two hours a night I am doing something. Always dreaming."

He became jittery like a child with an attention deficit disorder and poked the side of his cheek with the pencil. "Is this more childhood molestation dreams or is this something new? I read in the notes from your last therapist that you have nightmares often."

———

Thinking about the trouble I caused and all the guilt I felt, I snapped back, "I see someone has been doing their homework. Well, good for you, Doc."

"All right, Michelle I think it's time to end this. We aren't getting anywhere. I'll give you something to help with your sleep deprivation." He pulled out his prescription pad. "Take only one pill every night or else you will sleep for days. Hopefully, this will help."

I grabbed the prescription and rushed out of the office without saying a word. One more drug added to my extensive catalog. Behind closed doors, I was a down-low pill junky. I popped pills day and night just to remain normal. It became my only escape from reality. Missy wasn't the only one medicated from time to time. Prayer was no longer enough for me as I played the organ while being high for years.

I walked swiftly toward my car in deep thought. My emotions and hormones were on ten. I swung the car door open and climbed into my SUV.

Once inside, I doubled over. The pain squeezing my heart was too much to endure. My belly bounced on the bottom of the steering wheel. His baby was growing inside of me. I never wanted a pregnancy. But my birth control failed me.

I reached down in the zipper portion of my purse, scooping up two pills out of my Ziploc bag and popped them into my mouth. I closed my eyes again swallowing quickly. They melted like candy. I wiggled my tongue around, bouncing my head back to ensure that the pills went down smoothly.

Once they dissolved, I was in a different time zone in my mind—a zone that became familiar and frequent and would take away all the remorseful cares of this world. I was disturbed and needed to commune with God. I knew that, but once the pills kicked in, my vision was unclear.

♪ Lord, save me. Too zooted to move. I leaned back, reclined in my heated leather seat and took a drug-induced nap right in the parking lot of the mental health building.

One thing was for sure, I had an addiction and needed help. Maybe just maybe, I can take as many pills as possible so that this mistake in my belly can go away.

SIXTEEN

MISSY

My sermon was fire!

I waltzed back and forth on the church hardwood floors, giving the word of God and waiting for all that wanted prayer. It was my first Sunday as pastor. With the anointing of God all over me, I swept olive oil across the forehead of three new members who desired deliverance. The altar call was powerful, and the audience made a joyful noise unto the Lord.

"The word says let not your heart be troubled for I am with thee." My hands flung toward the sky in praise. I felt a powerful surge jumping up and down as God reached down to slap me high-five.

"Have you given your life to Christ?" I asked the three. They shook their heads in unison.

"God wants to use all three of you. He has a special plan for your lives. Do you agree?"

They all nodded.

"Repeat after me, God so loved the world that he gave his only begotten son and whosoever believe in him should not perish but have everlasting life."

I waltzed around them swinging my red-and-black robe with matching tippet from side to side imparting the love of God from my hands. My eyes moved around, becoming mindful of the camera angle. I felt like Juanita Bynum bringing fire and brimstone to the three individuals.

Mother Gaines stood from the front pew and screamed, "Hallelujah. Thank you, Jesus."

I looked into the cameras and said, "If you are out there in television land seeking the Lord, repeat this prayer with us."

The congregation knew that was the cue to stand. They had the option to come to the altar or pray at their seats. Hundreds of people pressed forward with their hands lifted moving to the front of the church. God met us at the altar as we prayed. I couldn't control myself as tears dripped in between my words. It's funny how in God's presence, anxiety didn't exist.

White lights signaled that my time was almost up and the cameras swerved around us. But it was hard to stop when God was moving. Some of the members gripped the altar, kneeling in reverence to Him while others bunched up closely in front of me. My dad was in the pulpit, stomping his foot, full of excitement as more people entered the aisles and made the walk toward the altar for prayer.

"The first three who came up today are ready for a change, and by the looks of all who are at the altar, we all want some form of change in our lives. Give it all to Him on this day. Tomorrow might be too late."

"Say it, gal," Daddy yelled, waving his hands.

Mother Gaines bobbed her head, yelling as if I was sitting right beside her. "Yes, you'd better say it, gal. Say it. Hallelujah."

Mother Smithfield looked down the same pew, whispering under her breath.

Mother Gaines shouted and bobbed even harder knowing that all eyes were on her. She and Mother Smithfield had their moments of bickering depending on the season. I became used to the back and forth while in church and I knew they would probably get started soon as Mother Gaines continued to cheer me on. "Let God use you, gal. Whoa, Lord. Thank ya, Jesus." She lifted her hands high.

Mother Smithfield jumped forward as if someone had pinched her on the arm. She called Mother Gaines a *sellout* because she always went extra hard in praise whenever I preached. She scooted up, mimicking her. "Say it, gal. Hallelujah." Lifting her hands and giggling while they dangled in the air. All the mothers laughed, holding hands up to their mouths as she demonstrated her moves.

I looked over with a stern look and started singing to ensure that I would drown out the laughter. We were still being recorded for live television.

Mother Gaines' eyes widened while she continued to yell louder than a soccer mom standing on the sideline of a championship game. "Get your eyes off me, Smithfield." She bounced her shoulders, responding to the words of the song. "Lord, yes. Sing, Chile." She clapped her hands.

Mother Smithfield scuffed the floor with her orthopedic shoes, trying hard to contain herself without reaching over to grab her. She looked straight ahead, still giggling like a child.

"Sing one more verse, gal.

"He is faithful, oh so faithful."

"Sang," Daddy uttered.

I stretched out each note while the crowd finished up at the altar and walked back to their seats. The final invocation began as the congregation came down from their spiritual high. I watched Mother Gaines rubbing her neck and looking over at

Mother Smithfield with threatening eyes.

"What is it, woman? Did you lose something over here?"

Mother Smithfield twisted her wig until it was back in place and raised her fist midair.

"Keep talking, you hear?"

"I wish you would," Mother Gaines woofed back. She slumped down, making her voice deep and raspy. "More prayer is needed on this row, Father. More prayer is needed. Thank you, Lord. Whew. Glory to your name."

Pushing up her sagging boobs, Mother Gaines made a great effort not to lean over too much further as her scoliosis and osteoporosis had her bent sideways. She reached in her white bow-shaped purse and pulled out a big piece of peppermint to settle the score.

She held out the peppermint crossing over Mother Agnes and said, "Have some, dear?"

Mother Smithfield probably needed the candy to assist with her glucose drop and tainted breath. Blinking her big brown eyes with her crooked eyelash extensions, she responded, "I guess."

She reached over the other side of Mother Agnes, snatching the peppermint out of Mother Gaines' hand. She popped it in her mouth, looking in the other direction with her arms folded across her chest. She was at ease as she rocked back and forth waiting for the service to end and probably thinking about her next bingo game.

"I knew that would shut her up," Mother Gaines said, holding her hand over her mouth, trying hard to keep her false teeth in place.

We made eye contact again as she became frozen. She leaned back like a child who was being silently scolded.

The church stood up to say the final words.

"Repeat after me," I said. "All praises, all glory, all honor belongs to the God of Israel forever and ever let the church say…"

"Amen," the church yelped back.

"God has spoken. Now let the church say amen."

"Amen."

Darryl played, "Oh, How I Love Jesus" while Michelle sat up in the balcony looking agitated.

I walked to the beat with the ministerial team on each side of me. I reached the back hallway, wiping my hands clean with my robe to greet every member.

Everyone continued to stand in place as the rest of the clergy members walked to the back.

The church lined up single file right after swaying to the music. Several members kissed and hugged going out the door. A frail woman walked up slowly with her hat tilted low below her nose. I admired her gray shoes with red bottom soles giving her a compliment.

"Nice shoes."

"Why thank you. May God bless you, my child," the woman said.

"God bless you also," I responded in a cheery voice, waiting for the women to move forward.

The flimsy hat tilted up in the air as her red lipstick glistened. She had long lashes with black eyeliner smeared below her eyelid. She winked as she puckered up, inching to kiss me.

I doubled back, realizing who stood in front of me. It was Olivia Wallace, my biological mother in the flesh.

My eyes burned. I clenched my hands together.

Her hands flounced up in my face. "Well hello, Passuh."

With a voice oozing with sarcasm, I replied, "Hello Olivia. Glad you could join us today. I hope the word moved you this morning." I tried to keep calm while others waited behind her.

She looked displeased at my expression as her fake lashes clumped together. "Why yes, my dear, it touched the very pit of my soul."

"I am glad." I winked back.

She grabbed my arm leaning close to my ear. "Today it's about the Lord, but tomorrow it will be about my loot. Don't make me take you and your daddy out like you all did that boy. I thought I would come and see my daughter preach since I will own the church too before it's all said and done."

I whispered back with confidence, leaning in as my top lip rested on her ear. "Jesus is my strength, so bring it."

She pulled back, laughing loudly, putting her hands on her hips, trying hard not to make a scene. She pulled her phone out of her designer purse, looking me up and down. The phone dangled in my face like a carrot being tossed in front of a rabbit's nose.

"Guess what, Passuh? You're on candid camera and the video inside this phone is my strength."

"Is that right?"

"Yes, that is right little girl. And before you know it, I will own this church, get my money, and help the police convict your Lil' BFF."

"Get out of God's house with this Olivia."

"Good day, little girl. I think I'll be seeing you real soon with my money, right?" She stepped up with a bounce and then leaned back imitating a southern drawl.

"You are evil."

"Don't get caught on video again, ya here."

I stood baffled waiting for the next member to step up. "Pastor, are you okay?" the member asked.

My heart was full of rage while swallowing deeply. I wanted to go after her and throw her in the trunk of my car. Driving her to an undisclosed area and throwing her in a ditch might be fitting for a witch. But instead, I fixed my face, tapped my right foot up and down, and continued to reach out my hands greeting members. "Why, yes. I am fine."

SEVENTEEN

NATALIA

The sun was shining brightly at the streets of Southpoint Mall. I was dressed for church wearing a purple two-piece suit and silver heels. But at the last minute, I decided to drive straight down Fayetteville Street instead of turning onto RTP drive. I wanted to treat myself to a matinee. The latest Jordan Peele horror movie was the talk of the town. My curiosity took control as I wanted to see what the talk was all about.

Based on the glorious weather, a movie seemed more suitable than going to church. Instead of sitting on an uncomfortable pew over two hours, a big barrel of popcorn with a cherry slush was more my speed for the moment. Besides, I had already heard a nine o'clock word from a preacher out of Atlanta on the Word Network. I received a good message entitled "God's in control." What could be more powerful than a title such as that? That was a word that quickened my soul and would carry me throughout the week.

I made my decision.

After the movie, the scent of buttered popcorn followed me outside. Remnants dripped onto my pretty suit along with the residue of yellow oil on the tip of my fingers. I sat down in a long green wooden chair placed in front of the theatre's *Now Showing* signs. Along with wooden chairs, the area had single metal chairs and tables, a large water fountain, clothing stores, and several restaurants along each side of the building.

Happy children ran in a circular motion around the diamond shaped fountain placed in the middle of the brick sidewalks.

Children of all ages threw coins in the fountain. They stuck their faces down admiring their own shadows while looking into the hazy body of water. I loved watching them play. Their cherub faces were moistened by the heat of the sun with mist bubbling on their cheeks.

I wanted to have children of my own one day. If I could only give birth to just one, my life would be complete. The Cheesecake Factory stood several feet away as the aroma of all the different foods drifted my attention from the children. I closed my eyes imagining a thick piece of Oreo Cheesecake with extra whipped cream and someone to share it with.

Before I realized it, I looked up and started to resent all the happy families around. The rapid beats of my heart lessened. *Why don't I have this type of happiness in my life?*

Loneliness engulfed me. Still, I couldn't pull my eyes from the families. I released a long sigh. Internet dating shouldn't be my only option these days to meet a good man. I do acknowledge my difficult personality and that is why the Internet became a vital tool and my haven for dating. I desired to be in a long-lasting relationship with someone who was loving, caring, and in need of a family.

After my mother's experience with my dad's infidelity and watching my two friends bomb on love, my exterior had an invisible guard plastered across my chest. With so many restrictions on the things that I would and refused to put up with, internet dating was the easiest. I couldn't seem to take my eyes off the children.

I was captivated by so many in one place at one time. One child stuck out the most. She was a Caucasian girl with long red hair. She looked to be around the age of five. You could tell she was a nuisance to her siblings as they ignored her. So instead of taking their rejection, she grabbed her big brother's hand and forced him to run with her. That's how I used to act towards Missy and Michelle when we were kids. No matter how much I got on their nerves, I always made them play with me. I sniffled getting filled with emotion and appreciating when life was so simple back then.

I put my head down and started scrolling through my online dating apps on my phone. Several alerts chimed. I was registered with quite a few. The latest popular app called Black Men in North Carolina was my favorite. It showcased single, harmless and hard-working men right in the triad area. I sifted through messages from potentials while smiling back at the children every now and again as my instant messenger popped open overtaking my screen.

CHOCOLATY 252: Well, hello lady.

HONEY 919: Hey there.

CHOCOLATY 252: Love the new pictures. Is your smile always that pretty?

HONEY 919: Why of course! Emoji smiling faces on the end.

CHOCOLATY 252: I am in Durham today. Can we hook up?

HONEY 919: Oh nice. Sure. I am at the Streets of Southpoint sitting right in front of the Cheesecake Factory. Would you like to join me for a bit? Are you nearby? I just love their Oreo cheesecake.

CHOCOLATY 252: Ha Ha. It would be my pleasure pretty lady. I love their Oreo Cheesecake too. If you are willing to share.

HONEY 919: Smiling emoji faces appeared again after his last comment.

I chatted with this guy several times before. I knew all about him. He traveled around the world just like I did with his ten-man team technology company making last month's Black Enterprise Magazine. He was all over social media getting accolades from major entrepreneurial organizations as he rose quietly to his fortune. Even with all his success, he was still single, never been married, with no children. A good prospect to spend a little time with over cheesecake.

I wanted the rest of my day to be memorable and I figured he might be the person to help me complete that task. Frank Thomas was his name. He was dark brown with sandy hair and big light-brown intriguing eyes. Forty-one, a little over six feet tall, and ex-military. Much older than my normal type, but he seemed quite stable with a very good head on his shoulders. From our previous conversations, I knew he loved his family and yearned to have children someday even if he had to adopt.

I fluffed out my natural hair with my big toothpick comb that I pulled out of my purse. I had to make sure it was full of bounce, ready to meet my new potential date.

I sat patiently under the sun. He appeared twenty minutes later standing right in front of me. I looked up at him as if I just laid eyes on a chocolate God as his skin shimmered. I felt paralyzed.

My jaw dropped lower every second.

His profile picture didn't do him any justice. Standing taller than a doorframe, he leaned up against the chair. I studied all his chocolaty goodness as if he was a biology assignment. No wonder he named himself chocolaty 252. He was originally from Henderson, North Carolina which was forty-five minutes away from Durham and the last three numbers on his profile was the area code of his hometown. He looked like a biscuit and molasses eating type that could move mountains with his fingertips.

I kept my legs crossed trying to gain composure. The three rules of anger management class kept me steady as I remembered our meeting chants that helped in other life situations.

Always make eye contact, leave out vulgar words, and remain cordial; no matter what.

He reached down and hugged me. I veered to one side hugging him back tightly. Aside from his chocolatiness, he was dressed nicely in slim fitting black jeans and a Polo dress shirt tucked in at his small waist.

"*Well, hello.*"

"Hello, Beautiful." He took a seat next to me and I swear even the way the man bent his knees had swag. He was a cross between the actor Blair Underwood and Pittsburgh Steelers coach Mike Tomlin. I finally picked up my lip when I noticed that it dropped again making it obvious that I was in sheer awe of his virility.

"What's up, Nat? How's it going?" He spoke with a country accent.

"I'm good. Glad to finally meet you." I patted his knee trying to keep my voice from cracking.

He smells so good. His cologne had me sniffling like a hound as the aroma captivated my nostrils. His skin soaked with moisture as if he'd just glazed his body with a full bottle of cocoa butter.

Man, looka here looka here.

He wore a faded haircut with a thin beard that looked freshly cut. I stared at his fingers as he moved closer.

I had a habit of judging men by how their fingers were kept. My dad always said if a man's fingertips were clean then that was a good sign, it meant he washed daily. But if dirty fingertips were present, water wasn't his friend. I took heed to that belief as I always found myself monitoring nails everywhere I went even on women. It was a fascinating circumstance that was true for most. My heart pounded with glee after noticing his nails were not only clean but shining from a touch of oil around his cuticles.

Oooh weeee, so he is the metrosexual manicure type. There is a God.

"I am so happy you came. You're just my type." I sat back with laughter.

"Is that right?" He looked into my eyes laughing along with me.

I couldn't stop blushing. Sinful thoughts filled my mind. *Oh, what I could do with you, sir.*

I had to control myself because the devil was nudging me on the shoulder. I clamped my mouth shut and crossed my arms.

He looked lasciviously at my legs. "You are just my type too, Nat."

Droplets of sweat trickled down my nose as I attempted to make small talk. He reached over without hesitation and kissed me dead on my mouth.

Lord!

It was the best kiss I had in years. Moist lips, good smelling breath, and clean fingernails. What a wonderful afternoon this was going to be. I remained surprised at all his good qualities. But then my untamed mouth started asking questions messing up the flow of things. "I have to ask, are you gay by any chance?"

His eyebrows lifted. "What the heck? No, I am not gay." He was now offended and became testy at my out of place question.

"Oh, well, I figured I would ask. These days you never know with some people." He sat mesmerized as the question fizzled a mental fire. I could tell that I made him upset. My usual. The man has only been in my presence for less than ten minutes and I have already ruined everything.

✻ He brushed it off quickly. "Let's go in the restaurant and get a bite to eat. Would you like to sit inside or outside sweet lady?"

I stood up grabbing his hand and swinging his arm around. "It doesn't matter, as long as I am with you."

He smiled as he seemed no longer insulted by my questioning walking towards the restaurant hand in hand.

I was elated. I hadn't had a date that went this smooth after saying something out of line in months. *Who says you can't find a good man on the internet?* I had a good feeling about this one. My heart felt as if it was melting all down my suit. He was incredible to me already.

EIGHTEEN

MICHELLE

I raised upright in my bed. Another bad dream to add to my journal. It scared me so much that I found myself scanning my bedroom. Indeed, it was just a dream. When I finally realized that I was still by myself, I sighed relief and fell back against the pillows. The nightmare included Tommy, a Glock, and several threats on my life. "You ruined me. You ruined me. Now it's time to ruin you!"

I contemplated picking up my pills. My body jolted with short throbs of pressure striking my right side. *Is this pregnancy or another urge?* The longer this baby stayed in my belly, the more I became attached. I just wanted this pregnancy to be over and done with so I didn't have to second guess where each pain came from. Thankfully, my first trimester was coming to an end. I gag more than two times daily with vomiting episodes that tried to take me under. Morning sickness was a beast. I didn't know how much more I could stand.

My phone buzzed on the nightstand alerting a new text message.

Hey, girl. This is Nat. I have tried to call you six times already. Where are you? Let's all meet up downtown for lunch today, okay. Love you, girl. Bull City Chicken and Waffles would be a great spot to meet.

I responded: *Awesome that was my restaurant of choice too* with several emoji faces laughing with tears running down their yellow smiley faces.

I swerved my body around to the edge of the bed holding my stomach with my feet hitting the cold hardwood floor. I had to do something to erase this urge. *Lord give me a word, please.* I picked up my Bible, shuffled through several verses, and came across the scripture of honoring thy mother and thy father. My J.J. poster from *Good Times* stared back at me hanging sideways. Memories were triggered of my childhood as I closed my eyes.

"Oh, Daddy! J.J. is my favorite! How did you know to get this for my birthday?"

"I know what my little girl wants from her daddy."

Another year of life. The big thirteen. Daddy was always good at finding the perfect gift. I adored watching J.J. from the show Good Times.

Every chance I could get I would sit in front of the floor model wooden sided television and laugh with my brothers. After my grand birthday party, Daddy helped with planting scotch tape behind the poster. He lifted my tiny body high up in the air to plaster my new masterpiece.

"So, did I do good?"

"Yes, Daddy. Just what I wanted." I smiled.

He swung me around in his arms pressing his lips against my cheek. I loved having my dad around. But he did things that a little girl like me just didn't understand at that age.

The following Monday, my mom took me to my yearly checkup. I had low iron. Blood was always drawn at each visit. We waited patiently for the results after the drawing of blood and a few shots were given.

The doctor entered the room holding a large clipboard with several pieces of paper attached. He stood at the edge of the exam room door with an abnormal stare.

"What is it, Doctor Ellis. Is everything okay?"

He inhaled. The raw words of, "Mrs. Hanks, Human Chronic Gonadotropin has been found in Michelle's blood.

"What is that?" I asked.

"You're with child," came out instantly.

My mother didn't respond right away. Her face changed colors as her light complexion cheeks turned pink. "She's thirteen... impossible."

"I'm sorry." He scribbled notes on his paper. "The nurse will be in shortly to speak with you."

My mother looked away. The veins in her arms were showing. She looked as if her blood pressure was rising. Tears were falling down her face. When the doctor left the room her lips mouthed, "Let's go home, Chile. I know who the daddy is."

She looked like she had a suspicion, but now she knew for sure.

My daddy had been laying his five feet nine and two-hundred-and-twenty-pound body on top of me since I was three years old. It started with brazing of my skin. Then forcible talks with Mr. Thing started at age seven. He worked his way up to full penetration by the time I turned ten. I tried to tell her years ago that daddy was hurting me and point to my pants. But she would always yell, "What are you talking about Chile? Do I need to take you to see that shrink again?"

We sat in silence all the way home as her station wagon puttered down Roxboro Road. When we pulled up to the front door of our home, she turned toward the passenger side and grabbed me, while unbuckling her seatbelt in a hurry. "You little slut, you. You've just ruined our lives."

"It's not my fault, Mommy. It's not."

"Your daddy was good to me." She slammed her hands down on the steering wheel, filled with emotion and crying in between her words. "He's going to have to leave us. Don't you realize what you've done?"

"I'm sorry Mommy. I thought this is what little girls were supposed to do. To listen to their parents."

She wiped her face and said, "If you ever tell a soul, I will break every little bone in your nasty little body. You hear me?"

"The man I called daddy disappeared after that day. I instantly become a victim of low self-esteem, verbal abuse from my mother, and arrested development. She tried to erase the memory of his presence. Within the next five years, she changed everything in our home. My poster now remained beside my bed nailed to the wall. I couldn't get rid of it despite what he did. It was the only thing I had left of *Good Times*.

My mother eventually became overprotective, not wanting me and my brothers to leave her sight. Now at age twenty-seven, we all still reside in our family home not having any desires to leave.

My eyes shuttered trying to erase the thoughts out of my head. Yellow fluid with an odor rose within my throat. Morning sickness bum rushed my esophagus not allowing me to finish my Bible reading. I ran to the bathroom not able to make it to the toilet as vomit exploded out of my mouth and onto the floor.

"Oh God, here we go again."

I flirted with the idea that pill popping might be the cause of some of my vomiting episodes. But the thoughts were dismissed because I no longer had control of my addiction. My habit ruled my entire universe. I swished my mouth with mouthwash. My weave was still in tack as I patted it down in the bathroom mirror but my eyes were bleary as if I could see my own personal demons appear before me. I moved my head back and forth for several minutes to shake all the emotions away. I had to get it together and not allow my troubled spirit to be noticed at our gathering. I tried to wipe up some of the mess I made, throwing up again from the smell. I was running late and I had to shower.

After getting it together. I drove like a bat out of hell to get to the restaurant on time. Then it dawned on me. Thinking about my past would usually take me on the yellow brick road to pill popping. Instead, my past made me think about my unborn child's future. I fought the urge after reading the Bible. *Now I know I can do it again.* I created a simple solution for a complex problem and his name is *Jesus*. I prayed that the pills dissolved in my body didn't do any damage. For some reason, I wanted to keep him. I felt attached as his foot kicked my side. The birth of this baby was going to be life-changing. For all of us.

NINETEEN

MICHELLE

The restaurant was packed with people standing around waiting to be seated. I glanced at the wall of photos of all the celebrities that had eaten here. Then I spotted my friends. They were sitting at a corner table near the door of the kitchen.

Everyone around them was swiping a cell phone.

"Hello, fabulous sisters. How is everyone?"

Their heads turned toward my voice. This was the first sisterhood gathering since the murder. Unfortunately, the only seat available at the table was right next to Missy. *Just my luck.* I knew I would have to hedge my words so that they wouldn't notice anything different about me.

"Hello," Missy said. Her eyes roamed the length of my jogger outfit. She stood up giving a halfhearted hug.

"You look amazing, considering all you've been through, sis," Natalia stated as she stood up, too.

She reached for my neck. Her hug was warm and needed. I felt alone and isolated. I had this huge secret that was doubly burdened by my pending fate in court. I swallowed hard. I swallowed pain, loneliness, and regret.

"Thanks." I slid into my seat and reaching for the sweating goblet of water in front of me.

"So how are you feeling? I've been worried about you. We haven't really talked lately," Natalia asked with a look of skepticism and fretfulness.

"I feel great. Fabulous as always." I cleared my throat, draping a napkin over my belly.

"Yeah, Nat told me about Olivia showing up at the police station," Missy said rolling her eyes.

"Yeah, an overwhelming experience I must admit," I said feeling edgy. Talking to one another was a struggle.

"I find it intriguing that she would have the nerve to go there knowing you have nothing to do with her money."

"She didn't care. Good plan, bad execution." Natalia grinned.

"Well, don't worry about her, she's just desperate for cash. She may be my biological mother on the state records, but all I see is an old crackhead searching for a hit. She's nothing and my dad is going to take care of it."

Natalia croaked as if she was bemoaning the fact that Olivia was bold enough to approach us. "I still can't believe she did that."

"Nothing surprises me anymore. She showed up at church Sunday as well with the same ole mess," Missy said picking up her napkin and placing it on her lap.

"Yeah, I bet that was something," I responded looking away.

Natalia bounced up in her seat changing the subject. "So, what's the latest on the case? And how are you balancing all of this?" By her facial expression, I could tell she was feeling that something wasn't right. She had a powerful gift of discernment and was tuning into my frequency.

I hesitated. "Well, let's not talk about all that right now."

Natalia put her elbow on the table and balanced her hand on her chin. "Why not?"

I changed the subject after recognizing her *I am about to go there* so get ready tone overshadowed her normal voice. I knew she was truly worried. As usual.

"So, Missy, how are you enjoying your new role as pastor?" Natalia asked.

"I was born for this, my sistah. I can't even begin to explain how I feel right now. It's all God." She threw her hands up as they high-fived one another.

Natalia looked back at me, she didn't seem at all convinced

by my Oscar-winning performance as she lifted her glass of water. "Okay, enough with the small talk," she said. "What's up with you Michelle? I know this gathering is hard for the two of you but something isn't right." She ruffled her napkin in frustration and dropped it on her lap.

Missy gave her the evil eye.

"We've been friends for way too long and I know when something is wrong. Spill it, Chelly." Natalia's eyebrows curved in.

I pulled out my utensils, placing them in front of me, and wiping them down with a napkin. "I'm just happy to be here and out of the county jail. Nothing's wrong." I'm sure the word *liar* was written across my face as Natalia never stopped with the questioning.

"Why can't you just enjoy the moment like a normal person?" I said trying to lighten the mood with a chuckle.

I was soaked with sweat knowing that Natalia was going to pull the truth out of me. *Not today, Lord. Please don't let me have to tell them everything today.*

A petite Caucasian waitress with pink hair bumped against the table holding a pencil and notepad in her hands. "Good afternoon, ladies. May I take your order?"

Natalia ordered for all of us. "Yes, we'll all have the chicken and waffles special, please." She handed the menus back to the waitress.

"Coming right up."

"Oh, and don't forget to bring warm strawberry syrup, please," Missy said looking away.

Natalia examined my eyes as I tried to ignore her.

"Spill it before God reveals it for you," she said.

I took a deep breath. My heart skipped. I hoped the startling news wasn't going to have Missy fall out of her chair. I exhaled deeply grasping my napkin and answered in a calm tone, "I'm pregnant. There, you happy now?"

"Huh?" Missy gasped with a look of horror.

"What... the... H...?" The surprise made Natalia lean her chair back into the wall.

"You heard me. And there you have it, folks."

"Pregnant? By who? You ain't had a man in about six years," Natalia said, wrinkling her nose.

My face became masked with mockery. "Yup, you're right, and neither have you. Last time I checked babies don't always have to be produced by *my* man. Any man with a penis can get the job done you know." I responded.

"Wait, what?" Missy yanked her head back in disbelief. "So, who did you get impregnated by?" She scowled at me with her lips poked out. I could see the imaginary light bulb flickering inside her head as she swallowed with a big gulp. "Is it... is it...

Oh God... is it... Tommy's baby?" she screeched.

I swallowed hard. "Yes," I answered with a straight face. "But, you said he made you get an abortion after the rape?"

"Wait, what? Rape? Okay, I'm really confused now." Natalia's eyes went back and forth trying to follow the conversation.

I paused for a moment. "He didn't rape me. I lied." I looked at Missy and said, "Please don't hate me."

"Shut the front door!" Natalia slammed her glass of water on the table. Water sloshed and pooled on the table.

"What?" Missy mumbled, putting her hands over her face.

Tears burned the back of my eyes. I looked away from Missy's eyes.

I didn't want to see her pain again.

"So, let me get this straight...he didn't rape you, it was all consensual, you got pregnant, and you kept the baby?"

"Didn't I say all that already, Natalia?"

Natalia glared. "So, did you kill him out of spite?"

All eyes had already been on me, but now they burrowed deeper.

Eyebrows cocked and lips parted as they waited for my response.

I swallowed. "I haven't figured that out yet."

Missy strummed her fingers on the table in disbelief.

"Killing him wasn't my intention. We were very good friends and I enjoyed being around him. It wasn't often that we got together sexually until about six months ago. I guess I didn't realize that I was angry with him when I stabbed him that night. I'm probably angry at every man I've ever met for that matter."

"Well, well... I guess you aren't 'Ms. Holier Than Thou' like I thought. I thought you loved me." Missy huffed crossing her arms.

"I just knew you were still a virgin. You could have fooled me." Natalia squealed slapping her hand on the table.

"Lord have mercy on my soul," Missy whispered holding her chest. "Missy I do love you. I hate telling you this."

"Well, you got a funny way of showing it, lady."

"Listen. Please listen. Tommy loved you too. He decided when we came back from Jamaica that he really wanted to take you seriously. It probably triggered some hidden feelings inside of me that I didn't even know I had until that night. I really can't explain it right now."

"How long has this been going on?" Natalia chimed in.

"I met him in Goldsboro at the music retreat ten years ago. So, ten years off and on."

"Ten years ago, and you never told anyone that the two of you were good friends with sexual benefits? Now you know you need a swift kick..." Natalia paused making grunting noises while reaching for her water. "I just don't understand why you felt it was okay to keep this from us. We are better than this type of stuff. This is starting to sound like an episode of Pastors of LA." She shrugged in nonchalance.

Missy's eyes were glossy once again from my negligence. I didn't know what to say to make it right. "Well, if it will bring any closure, he really loved you. I swear he did. He wanted to marry you."

Missy looked up with a love-struck glare. "He really wanted to marry me?"

"Yes. And once he had that set in his head, this baby became an afterthought."

"Well, ham sandwich." Natalia said looking as if she was pushing down the cursing demon. She gulped her entire glass of water within seconds as if she was playing to win in a shots liquor game. "Where's the waitress? Do they sell adult drinks in here? After hearing all of this, I need at least three mini glasses of Tequila." She plopped her arms on the table full of exhaustion as if she had worked a twelve-hour shift and had spent an hour in Zumba class.

I averted my eyes away from their disappointed faces and into the crowded room. Missy coughed and tapped her foot. "This is so unbelievable. I could reach across this table and choke you right now."

I reached into my bag and pulled out a box placing it at the center of the table. I was hoping it would be my saving grace from getting my butt kicked. "He was going to give you this. He asked me to hold it for him days before the murder."

Missy studied it for a moment before picking up the box and opening it up. She trembled at the ravishing engagement ring that sparkled brightly.

"I even helped him pay on it a few times when he ran short on money." I was running out of kind words to say.

Natalia pulled out a piece of gum from her pocket. "This story is going to be a best-selling novel. Where is Oprah's book club when you need them? Geesh."

I focused solely on Missy's eyes and said, "I didn't mean to hurt you, Missy. I do love you. We're sisters, no matter what. When I introduced the two of you five years ago, I had no idea he would start dating you. I swear I didn't."

Her fist pounded on the table. "Does all of that matter now? My best friend who I confided in about everything is now carrying my dead ex-boyfriend's baby?" Missy's expression was a solid slate of stone.

Natalia lifted her head up in the air and said, "You better be glad you didn't do that to me. Your pregnant behind would be kissing the cement on this floor."

˙ Missy sat up dignified, sipping her ice-cold water as if it was hot tea. She looked up at me. " So, all our fallouts over the years was about him, wasn't it?"

I didn't respond pushing the box closer to her.

"It's okay because you'll have to answer to God, not me." She continued to sip. "When you told me, he raped you right before the murder and charges were pressed, I knew it was a lie anyway."

"How so?" I said with surprise.

"You used the phrase statutory rape. We didn't know him as teenagers so it didn't add up."

I started thinking about the terms I heard my mother use around the house when she contemplated turning my dad in.

"My mother used that term after my dad got me pregnant. A habit I guess."

"Your dad got you pregnant too? Stop lying. Oh, this is getting really ridiculous." Missy sucked her teeth.

"I'm laying it all out on the table now. I have nothing to lose at this point. There is so much you don't know about me. All I can say is I'm sorry, sis."

Natalia asked, "So how far along are you?" "Going on three months in a week," I answered.

"Woo wee Chile. Ain't that about nothing." She replied.

Missy sat up straight grinding her teeth. We exchanged looks as our food arrived.

"What can I say? I'm a filthy, dirty, wretched soul who made a huge mistake. Can you please forgive me?"

Missy's eyes screamed brokenness, disappointment, and more pain. She looked as if she had just lost her best friend.

We poured syrup on every section of our plates cutting up our waffles in silence. "I don't have the energy nor the time to be angry with you. I have too many souls to win for God's kingdom including yours. He has got to handle this one." Missy poked at her waffle with force. "I feel sorry for you. Jail or these streets isn't a safe place to be for a person like you." Her tone signified that I needed to watch my back.

Natalia dropped her fork on her plate and blew her breath.

'The guilt of it all was beating me down more than her hands could ever do.

Missy grabbed the ring and stuffed it into her purse without saying a word. The two of them munched down their food hurriedly. Either they were hungry or they wanted to end our gathering just as bad as I did.

I stood up pushing my chair to the side not wanting to continue and said, "I'm having this baby. God has already forgiven me. I just need to forgive myself."

I pulled out a twenty-dollar bill throwing it on the table. My back turned abruptly with a forward march to the door. I held back my tears until I reached the outside. This was only the beginning of our end.

TWENTY

MISSY

Two Months Later...

Beanie traveled back and forth to Jamaica for short periods of time only to check on his mother and box things up to be shipped to Durham. We were making great strides together as I tried to erase my feelings for Tommy. It wasn't easy but I played it off well.

We pulled up to the church as he parked in the pastor's parking space. He tugged at my dress and said, "I have a surprise for you."

"Really. What is it?"

"You'll see when we get inside."

I looked at him starry-eyed. What could top the delivery of

one hundred roses to my office? Or being picked up by a limousine for an entire week? Or cooking breakfast, lunch, and dinner while I sit back with my feet up on my cozy couch?

I tried to pry the information out of him by reaching over and giving him subtle kisses on the neck but it didn't work as he climbed out of the car and moving to the other side to open my door. He treated me like royalty which helped with the grieving process.

When we entered the church, he walked me to my designated seat and kissed my hand. I watched him make eye contact with daddy and Mother Smithfield taking his seat in the front. Sister Monica came forth with the church announcements and after several dates given to add to our calendars she said, "We now have a special announcement by Deacon Beanie Anderson."

Beanie stood up and walked over to the podium.

"I have a dynamic testimony to give this morning church." His broad chest poked out of his blue three-piece suit. "Missy, will you please stand while I give my testimony?"

I stood as commanded wondering what he and daddy had up their sleeves as daddy smiled showing all his teeth while sitting beside me.

"Awhile back I met a woman that was visiting Jamaica for the first time. She was so beautiful, I wanted desperately to get to know her."

⁍ Several oohs and aahs rang out from the crowd. "Well, you know what? God blessed me to stay in touch with that beautiful woman and she is now the love of my life."

He held the microphone against his chest as several members yelled, "aah that's so sweet."

He pulled me down the pulpit steps to the front of the congregation. He spun me around to ensure that my eyes were solely on him while bending one knee, firmly planting it onto the floor. He gave a charismatic smile and said, "Missy Rochelle Jones...will you marry me?"

I put my hands on his face rubbing his goatee and mouthed one word. I wanted to be honest with him and tell him I wasn't ready to date anyone let alone marry someone. But the entire church awaited my answer. I couldn't let him down and I didn't want to see this muscle-bound Jamaican go ballistic on camera. I had no other choice with hundreds of people sitting in front of us. "Yes, yes, yes."

"They can't hear you, honey; what did you say?" He teased.

Tears dropped onto my shoes as I took deep breaths to say the lie one more time. "I said *yes*. Yes, Beanie Nathaniel Anderson, I would be honored to be your bride."

The congregation cheered, danced, and shouted unto the Lord for my newfound happiness as the musician played *Here comes the bride.*

Mother Smithfield grinned from ear to ear and screamed, "Hallelujah. She got a good one, Lord. Thank you, Father. The curse is broken."

Michelle sat in her seat of choice, the front row of the balcony. She looked down as I looked up. She clapped to the music with her pregnant belly protruding.

For a split second, I understood her need to lie as I was performing the same acts of deception as she did. But instead, I zoomed back into Beanie's eyes grabbing his head and kissing him passionately.

Beanie pulled a white gold ring out of his pocket. The diamonds swirled in a circular motion with one large diamond placed on top. The sparkle was enough to cause blindness as I admired the clarity. He escorted me back to my seat allowing the service to continue.

I leaned back in my chair rolling my shoulders trying to relax. My anxiety started to fester.

God... can you hear me? Please be my peace. That baby that Michelle is carrying should have been mine. Lord, please heal my heart.

TWENTY-ONE

NATALIA

Another Sunday afternoon gathering of the minds. It was the annual Fifth Sunday Jubilee Fish Fry. A grand celebration was also underway for Missy and Beanie's engagement. Southern sides were catered from Bull City Pitmasters and a big three-tiered cake sat at the end of the food table. Pastor Jones wore his "The Man" apron while burning on the grill. He smiled continuously enjoying the packed yard filled with the Mt. Zion congregation and visiting churches. He walked in and out of the building carrying packs of fish in his arms.

I finally had the courage to bring Frank around the others as things seemed to mesh well with our new friendship. I couldn't help but pinch myself every time I looked over at him. The air was crisp with minimal sun.

But the sky was clear and it was a perfect day for a fish fry.

Michelle jumped from table to table helping to set up with her visible baby bump. She looked beat down from the pregnancy but had no problem putting on her usual performance while around us.

Frank was introduced to everyone that wanted to know him as Missy ran up to meet him.

They shook hands while Missy spouted. "Such a pleasure to meet you. I've heard so much about you."

"Nice to meet you as well Pastor Missy," He responded.

Missy pointed over to Beanie. "That's my fiancé sitting over there. I will introduce the two of you as soon as I get the meatballs out of the oven. Would it be okay if I borrowed your lady for a few seconds so she could help me carry some of the food outside?"

"Of course." Frank smiled.

I followed behind Missy, getting Michelle's attention to come along with us.

"Why did you do that? I have nothing to say to her."

"You two need to talk whether you like it or not Missy. This has gone on way too long."

When we reached the dining hall area, Missy turned to ask, "How's the baby?" She looked down with envy.

"He's doing well."

Missy reached into the stove grabbing the meatballs with force not having much to say. At times, she seemed to do her very best at loving Michelle as God would want her too. But you could tell by her body language that her flesh was telling her something totally different.

"Well, the gang's all here." Pastor Jones shouted from behind the kitchen door. My three favorite children. What you all got going on?"

"Just some chicken pineapple meatballs to go along with all that good grilled food you have out there," I answered.

"Uh huh. The best meatballs in Durham." He mumbled.

"What are you doing down here, Daddy? I don't see any fish in those hands." Missy asked.

"I'm going to the office for a brief meeting. I have someone waiting for me. I will be back on the grill in a few minutes."

We moved around the kitchen getting more paper plates and napkins. A few minutes later, we heard two voices in a heated argument that could have awaken the dead.

We all froze as the voices moved closer toward our location.

Pastor Jones turned the corner with his hands flaring up and a paper bag cradled in his armpit.

Olivia Wallace followed behind him. She was dressed in a black catsuit and high-heeled ankle boots looking like she was ready for the club.

Pastor Jones held onto the brown paper bag in his hand with a firm grip.

"What's going on, Daddy? Why is she here?" Missy asked.

"I asked her to meet me yesterday to get her money, but instead she shows up today with all these church folks in the backyard." He eyeballed Olivia. "But I'm gonna give you some of what I promised… then you got to go."

"Don't do this," I said. "Paying her is not going to make her stay away. She just likes to be seen and run her mouth."

Olivia batted her eyes, seemingly not concerned about anything else but that paper bag. She waited patiently for the exchange.

Pastor Jones seemed embarrassed that he had all three of us to witness his unethical behavior still holding the bag against his chest. "This ain't all of it but I will get the rest to you in a few weeks. I'm a man of my word." He continued to look at her eye to eye.

"Don't give her a dime, Daddy, please. Don't do this. You promised you would try and do the right things from now on. Please, Daddy." Missy interjected.

He scratched his brow. He wouldn't take his eyes off Olivia. "I have to, gal. This is the only way I can get some sleep at night. I can't keep dealing with my past. I made a crazy vow to this woman, so I must be a man about it. If I don't, she will haunt us for the rest of our lives."

"Yeah, but with the churches money Daddy? Please don't get yourself in trouble, please."

"You got that right, Henry," Olivia confirmed snapping her finger.

"Daddy, please. Do the right thing for once. The Godly thing."

He threw Missy a look that meant *be quiet gal. God doesn't need to hear all of this.* "I have twenty-five thousand dollars in this bag until I can get more cash. Take it and go."

Olivia looked him up and down with an appalled glare. "You and your nice church, nice cars, nice clothes... you ain't hurting for nothing. You have everything you ever desired due to my sacrifices for that brat of a child we had together. This isn't what we agreed upon. I gave up my only child, my life, and kept hush of all your messy church secrets. You think that chump change is going to keep me quiet? This is all the thanks I get?"

He scratched his forehead.

"You stole my life from me. I deserve more than this kind of treatment when I come around." Olivia blurted.

"Well, considering I now have the note he signed... your agreement is null and void," I uttered.

All eyes were on me.

Olivia's mouth dropped open. She quickly composed herself and demanded, "Give it back before I beat it out of you."

Pastor Jones grinned, wrapping both arms around the bag of money even closer and pushing her back in place with his hip. He danced around with the bag as if he found a new tango dance partner. He caressed it, smothered it, and kissed it making it his imaginary human body blow up doll. Holding it felt warmer than holding his second wife who barely came to any of the church functions.

"Olivia, you may scare everyone else but you don't scare me. Don't give her jack Pastor." I said.

He walked back into the study.

We followed him with Olivia on our heels.

He swung the metal safe door open that had other stacks of cash, bent down, and emptied the bag right in the center. He slammed the metal door shut standing straight up and throwing his hands in his apron pockets. "Well, I guess my name is finally cleared from all of this."

"Excuse me, Henry?" Olivia folded her arms.

"You don't have any evidence of ever making an agreement with me. It's now my word against yours and it won't hold up in a court of law. No money for you, dear."

"You think you can end the deal just like that, huh? It doesn't work that way, Henry. I've waited twenty-seven years for this."

Olivia spat, "I did what I was supposed to do. Now it's time for you to do your part. You better give me my money."

"Money? *What money?*" He laughed.

She rambled frantically through her belongings hoping that she could find the note somewhere deep down in her Coach oversized shoulder bag. She pulled out several small pieces of paper throwing them on the floor searching hard for the agreement.

Once she realized it was officially gone from where she thought she had put it, she yelled, "What's your name?"

"Natalia. N.A.T.A.L.I.A. Shall I spell it again for you?"
"Hum... you just wait."

"Wait for what? You're just mad because you misplaced your meal ticket and it landed smack dab in my hands. Don't get mad at me because of your careless mistake. I guess that'll be the end of your show-stopping appearances, huh?"

She shook her fist in the air. "Oh, I have a trick for all of you. I'm giving the video to the police as soon as I leave here. You're all going to regret this." She stomped her boot several times and kicked her leg out toward Pastor Jones as he jumped back avoiding her tiny feet.

"Watch it there, gal." He grinned, enjoying every moment of her sunken state.

"You people think that I am playing, don't you? When I get

done, you will be good and ready to give me all my money and the deed to this church, Henry Cepheus Jones. Or else I will destroy all of you."

Cepheus?

Pastor Jones laughed uncontrollably, slapping his knee. "Okay, Sugga. Without that paper, King Kong ain't got nothing on me." He quoted Denzel Washington's famous line from the movie Training Day ushering Ms. Bag of Bones to the door.

Olivia didn't budge. "Trust me, I'll find a way to get that agreement back and get my money." She then pierced her eyes at me and said, "Watch your back, nappy head. We have unfinished business to take care of. See you in the streets."

I bent over with laughter. "Yeah right. You already missing teeth. You don't want to go there with me because I can easily help you with free removal of the rest."

"Alright woman, get out of here. You hype up Natalia if you want to and I just might be preaching at your funeral." Pastor didn't flinch as he dared her to utter another sound. "Now get on up out of here and leave us be."

She licked her lips, moistening her lipstick and smiled before

walking briskly and trying her best to balance wobbling from her high riding boots. She made grunting noises out the door.

"Who does she think she is?" I asked.

"Yeah God. With my three Lil' Warriors positioned for

battle, I think she made a good choice by leaving quietly." Pastor Jones snickered.

"I know she's going to retaliate. What do we do when she does?" Michelle asked with her hands posted on her belly.

"God will prevail, Chile. We do what we always do...pray without ceasing. Or as my mama used to say, swing first and ask questions later."

We chuckled in unison.

"I got other debts to pay, so now that I don't have to pay her, I am feeling really good about this thing." He brushed his pants off, making sure he was once again presentable to the public.

Missy put her hands on her hips. She looked like she wanted to talk to him but paused and walked back to the kitchen. Pastor Jones walked out the door all smiles as if he had conquered a giant with his bare hands.

What in the world is going on with him besides that agreement? Who does he owe? There was something else hidden besides a handwritten non-notarized agreement. Something just wasn't adding up as my discernment sent chills down my spine. I just pray that whatever it is, it won't involve Missy.

TWENTY-TWO

MICHELLE

Downtown Durham...

The talk of the town was the video. Olivia made it go viral just as she promised. I could hear people around me whispering and shocked by my actions. It was the last thing needed to be leaked to the public as it made national headlines. I was pretty sure it swayed everyone's opinion of my innocence and I had completely given up the fight.

It was 8:45 a.m.

I studied the clock hanging high on the courthouse wall.

It seemed to move at a faster pace than I wanted it to. It was a colossal piece that could be spotted more than fifty feet away.

All I could think about was the time that would be taken away from my life, family, friends and unborn child.

Time. I needed more time.

Time. It is the one thing that I've taken for granted.

All the hours, minutes and seconds I've spent going around in circles with Tommy, pills, and lies could have been precluded and used more productively. But instead, I wasted the most precious years of my life. Many years of quenching my addiction and sexual desires consumed more than half of it.

I sat on a bench outside of the courthouse waiting for my attorney to arrive before walking into the courtroom. Instead of taking everyone through the grueling trial process that could take years, I entered a plea of guilty.

Lord knows I don't want to have my baby in jail. I tossed my hands down in disgust waiting patiently as the clock continued to move.

"Hello, Ms. Hanks. I think the court will approve your plea today. But the prosecutor would like to make a recommendation. I'm sure since you have a clean record, they might show some favor."

I noticed the clock again. "Okay."

"I think we could have beat this case. But if this is what you want, it's a good thing I guess."

"Yes, I do believe it is."

"The media is almost unbearable outside and there is a woman's group out there with your name on their signs. Do you know all of these people?"

"Somewhat. But it doesn't matter. They are about helping women like me get out of this mess. I guess after today they will realize their help isn't really needed."

"Unfortunately."

"I've let everyone down including that group. I wish they would realize that I deserve to be in here. I've hurt so many people and I've lost my best friend."

"Yea, I am sure this is taking a toll on you and your family. But listen, I am going to request that everything is delayed until you have your child. That is the least I could do. I know you don't want to have your baby in prison."

"No, I don't. You must be reading my mind. That is so kind of you."

He smirked. "I just wished you would have trusted me on this one."

"My decision had nothing to do with not trusting you Mr. Smith. I'm a bad person and I should not be allowed to walk the streets with all my issues. I'm a liar, a thief, a pill abuser, and a horrible friend. My time in prison will force me to get closer to God. I need this more than you know."

"There are so many other methods you could use to get

closer to a higher calling instead of jail time. But I get it. I'm pretty sure you will appreciate everything being delayed so you may have that baby in a normal hospital, right?"

"Yes, I believe I will."

"Good. You'll want to know your baby before going in. Now let's go inside."

We walked in side by side and moved to our designated space. My church family sat right behind me. I leaned back in my chair winded by the unknown locking eyes with the judge. I didn't tell anyone with the exception of the attorney about the plea. They would find out all about it soon enough. I hope a box of Kleenex will be available. No one is going to agree with me on this one.

My attorney tottered closer whispering in my ear, "Don't let their faces scare you. We got this." He assured me with a shoulder nudge.

I leaned forward with my weave mangled on each side and said, "If you say so."

———

Discussion of my plea acceptance went back and forth amongst the attorneys and the judge. It was determined within twenty minutes that my plea would be accepted with the charge of Involuntary Manslaughter. The prosecution recommended five years. My attorney fought back and an agreement was reached. I was going to be given the maximum of eighteen months. The judge agreed to postpone further action until after the baby was born. The word traveled fast. The advocacy group outside packed up their *Free Michelle* signs and went home. They probably felt betrayed. They wasted energy in the humid downtown streets fighting for a woman that didn't want to fight for herself.

I was eventually going to prison for killing someone per my request. Not only did I want to free myself from the judgment of the world, but I hoped that time away would also allow my friends to forgive me. I looked up at the clock. I can no longer waste time with my sinful acts. I gave it all to God knowing that he is the author and finisher of my faith. *I surrender all.*

TWENTY-THREE

NATALIA

After the plea...

" "Hello?"

"Hello, Natalia."

"Hey, Michelle. I am so happy to hear your voice. Are you okay, honey?"

"No, I'm not. I'm so sorry. I am so, so sorry," she wailed.

"Honey, you've got to make it through this. No need to apologize to me."

"I let everyone down."

"Sweetie *Black Girls Rein* and everyone else will get over it. We are not your judge. You did what you felt was right. You need to pray about this thing."

"Okay, is this Natalia I'm talking to or Missy? Did you just say something about prayer, sis?"

I hissed.

"Well, I have learned to do it more myself too. I realized after all of this, that we need prayer more than ever and we can't sit around waiting for Pastor Jones or Missy to do it for us. You know what I mean?"

"I don't have any problem praying for myself. I just feel that God has forgotten about me, I know He has. Why did he pick me to go through this?"

"I used to ask that same question when my mother died. But Pastor Jones once preached when we were little kids on the topic, Why not you? You remember that?"

"Yes, I do actually remember that sermon. I just don't have any fight left in me, that's all."

"Well, you are pregnant you know. Being pregnant and going through all this, who would have the energy to fight right about now anyway?"

"My baby will be here soon. I don't know what I am going to do when I have to leave him and go to prison. He needs his mother."

"Maybe this is all a test or maybe God is giving you more time to bond with your baby. Think of the positive side of it all.

I know there are some positives hidden somewhere in all of this."

I felt like a new creature in Christ after witnessing her entire downfall. I strived to help women in her situation more and more. I didn't want to go against her decision to plea bargain with the system. But I still rallied behind her to continue having a voice. She allowed the world to hear her voice. It was just the opposite of what we all desired for her. But in the end, it was her voice that mattered, not ours.

"I just feel like dying, sis. This baby is the only reason I didn't push a bullet down my throat."

I ingested her words deeply allowing God to now control my temper as I lowered my tone. I couldn't believe she was talking like this. How did she fall this deep into depression without us knowing? But then again, we've never killed someone before, so we don't know the signs.

"I need you to stop talking like this Michelle. You are moving towards a path of nowhere with this mindset. You are fearfully and wonderfully made. Don't you realize that? I will not allow you to go out like this. I'm coming over to your house right now."

Since the murder, Michelle and I grew closer. She didn't mind telling me the truth about her childhood, her lies, her addictions and her desires for her unborn child. I had to help her through this. I was the only one left that would listen. She had to overcome sooner than later.

She mumbled. "Thank you. I probably need the company."

"Oh, you are more than welcome my dear friend. I am on the way as soon as I render a prayer."

There was a long pause. I guess my words were sinking into her head.

"You still there, Michelle?"

"Yes, I am. Did you say a prayer?"

"I didn't stutter. Are you listening?"

"Yes."

"Good."

"Wait. I have something else to ask of you sis before you start?"

I held the phone closer to my mouth gearing up to hear another confession. "I'm listening."

"I want you to take my son when I go to prison. Deep down, I just feel that you would be the perfect mother for him while I am away."

The phone dropped to the floor as I pulled my hands over my lips.

Michelle's voice could be heard faintly from the phone as it landed face down on the carpet.

"Hello Natalia, are you there?"

◀ I dropped to my knees. My hands jerked while picking the phone up.

"Yes, I'm here. I don't know what to say."

"Don't say anything right now. Just think about it for a little while and let me know how you feel in a few days. I really need you to do this for me."

"Well, what about your mom taking the baby?"

"Come on Nat. She couldn't raise me without getting hurt so why would I allow her to raise my child?"

"I understand. It's not anything I need to think twice about. I will do it on one condition... Promise me that you won't take him away as soon as you're released. Let's work on some form of transition. I know it's going to be hard for me to give him back. I always wanted a baby boy." My voice cracked as emotions twirled.

"Deal."

My enraptured state superseded over my tough exterior. And then it happened. I began to pray. I wanted to pray for her, for myself, and for the baby. A fervent prayer is what we needed at that very moment.

I slowly paced my words. The spirit filled me immediately while drenching my tongue with power. I didn't even realize I could pray like this, with such authority. I knew my prayers were going straight into the ears of The Master.

Michelle mumbled a few *yes Lord* and *do it God* in between each sentence. I lifted my hands in praise going deeper into a spiritual realm that I had never experienced. Michelle's tragedy brought on my deliverance. The prayer continued to belch forth as my voice lifted higher and higher unto the Lord. By the time I got to the end, I could barely mumble amen as I felt hoarse and tired.

"Michelle, I want you to know that I am so honored that you chose me. I will love him unconditionally. Thank you for trusting me. I am on my way over so that we can chat in person."

"I love you, sister."

"I love you, too."

TWENTY-FOUR

MISSY

The next day...

♪"So, what was the urgency to have dinner here?" I asked.

I swiped Natalia's arm with a love tap as her other hand held up a wine glass to my glass in a motion of cheers.

"Last night Michelle called me with some very exciting and unexpected news."

I crammed a piece of chicken breast in my mouth listening attentively. "Okay. What did she say?"

"She wants me to take the baby when she goes to prison."

The chicken swirled around filling my cheeks as I paused in the middle of biting down. I needed a sip of that wine she was having but instead, I tipped my glass halfway before putting it back down quickly. "What?"

"Yes, she wants me to have legal guardianship until she gets out of prison."

My eyes drooped. I didn't want to come off as a hater. *What would Jesus do?* "Oh, I see. Well, have at it."

"Missy, don't be like that. I want us all back together again. We are family."

"You can't be serious."

"I am dead serious."

"I don't want any part of helping her and that child. I have a right to be angry. She slept with someone I truly loved."

"Missy, you are moving on and getting married to someone else. Let it go."

"That isn't a guarantee. I am not in love with Beanie. I am not in a rush to lock down with him yet."

"Then why are you wearing his ring?"

"Because I can."

"That is selfish, Missy. Real selfish."

"How dare you belittle my feelings. Have you ever been in love before?"

"Not really."

"Well, hush then. You have no idea what I'm facing."

"I am sure you are worried about what your church is going

to say if you don't stay with him. Sounds like another *Cepheus* move if you ask me. Always worried about what the church folks will say or think."

"Don't say my daddy's middle name out in public, please. It's hideous."

We laughed.

◄ She doubled back at my response, "Just think about it, okay." "I have and the answer is still *no*. Do your thing."

I tapped my nails against my glass remaining pleasant as she looked back in disgust. "Sorry, it won't be any angels rejoicing at this one. I will not be having a Kumbaya moment with Michelle and Tommy's baby."

Natalia seemed to sense it was time to change the subject. It was a losing battle for her and Michelle in my mind. We spent hours reminiscing on our experiences throughout the last six months. From murder to engagement, to the plea; so much has happened in our lives.

Natalia seemed brand new and more relaxed now that she chose a new pathway. It was amazing to see her smile and laugh without a care in the world.

We left the restaurant stuffed from the wide variety of meats that were shared from the poultry platter we devoured. North Carolina's unexplainable weather change struck again. It was winter but yet eighty-five degrees. We were overdressed pulling off coats and hats and carrying the items in our hands.

I eased my hand into my purse searching for my keys. I shook it up and down waiting for a jingling sound but I could not feel them touch my fingers. "I think I left my keys inside the restaurant. I'll be right back."

Natalia leaned against the passenger side car door. "Okay hurry up. It's hot out here. I'm too pretty today for winter sunburn." We both laughed again.

When I returned to the car the unthinkable left me in a frozen trance.

Natalia fell to the pavement in slow motion with Olivia clenching her neck.

She pulled her shoe off and grabbed the side with the heel pouncing onto Olivia's arm. They bumped up against the car scratching the exterior across the side door.

"Oh my God! Somebody call the police." Onlookers clicked on their cellphone video buttons to capture the footage instead of calling the authorities.

"Someone please call the police." I scrambled in my pocket and purse patting all around looking for my cellular device.

Natalia hammered her hand up and down nonstop. She was getting the best of her hollering back at her with a deep tenor choir boy tone.

"You messed up when you came for me old lady."

I mustered the strength to pull her back feeling reluctant to interfere as I wanted Natalia to do everything I couldn't do as a woman of the cloth. But if I didn't stop it soon, Natalia was going to kill the woman with her bare hands. She threw the shoe down and started swinging her palm across Olivia's cheeks. Before each slap across the face, Natalia mumbled a word or two after each blow.

"You... thought... you could... hurt me... you devil... I bet... you won't... ever... come for me... again."

She straddled her down sitting on top of her thin waist.

Blood cascaded out of Olivia's mouth like a water fountain as she laid with her hands stretched to each side with labored breath. Olivia whispered with a loud hack of spit flying out of her mouth, "Let me go nappy head."

A large crowd gathered around. People from every restaurant on the Briar Creek strip inched closer to watch the beat down making oooh noises after every hit. Several minutes later the police hurled through splitting the crowd down the middle. Officer Taylor charged grabbing Natalia's arm and pulling her to the side of the pavement. I recognized him from the night of the shooting when I ran from the church as our eyes met.

"Well, if it isn't Missy Jones," he chuckled.

"Nice to see you again, officer. Glad you remembered my name." I scoffed.

"How could I forget you? We call you the long-legged track star down at the precinct. The way you had us running that night of your boyfriend's shooting, we will never forget your name."

I stood with a blank stare.

"You even ran me back into shape that night." He laughed at his own joke. "Glad to see you doing well. How's *That Church Life* going?"

"It's going well, sir. Thank you for asking."

He pointed at the ground as Olivia squirmed around attempting to get up. "Now what do we have going on here?"

"This old ratchet hag came after me. I need you to arrest this woman." Natalia said, composing herself.

"Huh?" The officer shrugged.

"Yes, believe it or not, sir. She pulled up in that beat-up truck over there, jumped out running in my direction, and attacked me for no reason." Natalia pointed to the red 1960's Ford truck parked in the middle of the parking lot.

An onlooker stepped forward and re-played the video for the officer's review. "She is telling the truth officer. Look at this," the stranger said.

Officer Taylor assessed the video and then looked back at Olivia. His face wrinkled as he looked surprised to see a lady her age on the attack.

Natalia stepped over Olivia, grabbing her shoe.

Olivia scrunched her face in pain trying once again to stand up on her own. Her legs rocked and her face was full of scratches. Her arms looked like a darting board as Natalia's heel did a number on them leaving several holes and gashes.

"State your name, ma'am."

She spit blood out of her mouth and said, "Olivia Wallace."

The officer apprehended her pulling out a set of handcuffs and throwing them across her wrist. He groaned at her behavior. "You out here in a ritzy part of town fighting with young folks, huh?"

"Ugh" She moaned from pain.

"What you should be doing was sitting down in one of these fine dining establishments enjoying your senior citizen's discount not fighting innocent people. Shame on you, lady."

"Whatever," she whispered, holding her hands steady.

"Now look who has a video to expose all over social media. Facebook is going to love this one." Natalia tittered with a low voice as the officer went inside his car to research Olivia's name.

Olivia throttled her body forward trying to get at her again with the only part of her body that was free, her legs. She kicked them around not being able to move like she wanted to due to the cuffs strickening her body.

When the officer came back, he moved in closer to Olivia monitoring her condition. None of the hits were considered life-threatening and he knew there was no need to call the paramedics. But he did ask several questions, checked her vision and pulled her closer to the police car.

His partner pushed her inside the car as he stepped over and asked, "So what agreement is she talking about that you supposedly stole. What money is she speaking of? She is talking in fragments over there."

"Sir, she is a very sick woman who has come to our church on several occasions begging for food and money. We don't know her personally and we didn't realize she was a savage from the streets. It looks like drugs have taken a toll on her mind, sir."

I nodded my head in confirmation. "I think my friend should press charges against this old soul because we have done all that we could do to help her and she still continues to harass all of our members. We don't know what you are speaking of concerning an agreement. We didn't make any agreement with this woman. She is just a homeless old lady seeking attention." I said folding my arms with contempt holding in my laughter.

The back door remained open as Olivia whaled, "I got your homeless woman you brat..."

"Quiet ma'am. I know a begging crack head when I see one

and the video has convinced me enough. You need to leave those drugs alone."

He looked back at us as Olivia jumped up and down full of rage in her seat.

"See look at her officer. Something is wrong with her." Natalia moaned with a facetious tone.

The officer took our side and said to her, "These are two highly respected women in the church and I know they don't have a reason to make up such a story as this. Aside from the lumps on your face, I doubt you will bother them again." The officer teased, grinning at Natalia as if he wanted to say out loud *nice job, Mike Tyson.*

Olivia pushed the police car door kicking the door handle with her tiny foot. Her rage was now on a whole new level as she cursed at the other officer standing beside her.

"Hey, get your feet down off the vehicle ma'am. Haven't you caused enough damage for today? Joe, call someone to tow her truck away and let's get ready to take her in."

"Shut the hell up and let me go home." Olivia continued to kick.

"All is well, ladies. We got this one. Until we meet again." The officer tipped his hat and pushed her legs into the car with exertion slamming the door behind them.

Natalia picked her purse off the ground, reaching into the

side zipper, grabbing the agreement and flashing it in the air.

As the car moved forward, Natalia held her hands out in front of her and ripped the frail piece of paper into a million pieces. She made sure Olivia took notice as she pranced around with the torn paper releasing into the wind one by one.

Olivia's eyes stretched from the side window gawking back with a deep frown. You could hear Olivia trying to bump against the secured door of the police car as it sped away.

I looked at the shoe placed in Natalia's other hand. The heel was snapped in half with the other piece of it sitting on the side of the car.

We exploded with laughter.

"I am going to put this in the back of her truck so she can have it for a souvenir. Something to remember me by. That woman is crazy for real."

She dropped the shoe in the truck and leaned into exchange a playful hug. "Thank God *Shoe Show* is in walking distance."

"I know right." I giggled.

"Let's do some serious shoe shopping, shall we?"

TWENTY-FIVE

MICHELLE

I was rushed to Duke Hospital from the OB-GYN clinic due to complications with my blood pressure and gestational diabetes. Micah Andrew Hanks was born at 5:08 a.m. early one glorious Sunday morning. He entered the world with a roar, making everyone around him aware of his arrival by his strong lungs blasting lengthening cries that could be heard outside of the delivery room.

Duke Hospital had another historical moment to add to their catalog of babies.

I was elated to finally meet him. The doctor pulled him out placing him on a steel baby table and cutting the umbilical cord. The other members of the medical team cleaned him up and handed him to me. I held him high with both hands. I could not stop looking at him. He was beautiful.

"It's a boy." Doctor Ellis said, smiling back at me.

I didn't use any pain meds to get him here. I went straight cold turkey through labor and stuck to it for over nine hours. The pain was beyond excruciating but being an ex-pill junky, it wouldn't be wise to put any form of substance into my system. I didn't ever want my addiction to come back again. I had been clean since the beginning of my second trimester.

His body was long as all eight pounds fit perfectly into my arms. His chubby cheeks and curly hair were a sight for sore eyes as his toes stuck out of the hospital baby blanket that coddled him.

I couldn't take my eyes off him. He was the most beautiful form of life that I had ever seen.

"He is so precious." My mother said standing beside me.

"You think so?" I asked.

"Yes, he is, daughter. Yes, he is."

He smelled like honeydew being served on a spring morning on an exotic island. I loved everything about him. His little hands. His tiny collapsed ears, and chubby toes. His caramel skin shimmered. The Lord had been with me all the way. From what the doctors could tell so far, he was overall healthy.

We had all changed tremendously after the murder. We grew

into women with a purpose and with powerful testimonies in less than a year's time. Missy was still angry. But Natalia and I had a bond that was even stronger than before.

"Would you like to hold him?" I asked my mom.

"Of course."

She grabbed him full of joy as she rocked him back and forth. "Yes, he is truly beautiful," She grinned widely looking down at him.

I thought about the cost of telling the truth. So far so good. It didn't take everything away from me as I expected. Instead, the truth gave me a free spirit. I had a lot of healing to do and a lot more truths to reveal. But most of all, I had Micah Andrew Hanks to live for.

———

The doctors were now allowing two people at a time to come in and see the baby. They kept him swaddled in a baby bed with other infants down the hall from me. A few hours later, they brought him back in the room with me. Pastor Jones and Natalia were the first two to visit.

"Now look at that. He got a head full of hair." Pastor Jones touched the top of his head with his finger.

"Yes, he does. I just love those Obama lips poking out at me." Natalia said with glossy eyes.

For the first time ever, Natalia showed emotion other than anger and sarcasm in front of us. It had been a long journey of transformation for her, too. With God's help, she now showed sincere signs of love, happiness and a whole lot of thankfulness toward me and my child.

I knew she would be the perfect person for the job as she mouthed, "Thank you, sis. You will never know what this means to me. He is just what I wanted for Christmas."

TWENTY-SIX

NATALIA

Frank and I arrived on the church grounds for noonday prayer. Michelle allowed me to babysit so she could get some sleep. Frank enjoyed helping me from time to time with the new bundle of joy. Each chance he could get off from work, he made an effort to spend time with me. Having him around while I practiced motherhood was a good thing.

He walked in with the baby carrier lifted high as we made our way to the altar. There were several other individuals already in place with their heads down praying silently. Pastor Jones greeted us at the door.

"Well hello, beautiful people. Look at Lil Micah. The next preaching man in the family. A fine little mocha brown baby, isn't he?"

"Yes, I suppose he is."

"I just knew he would be light like his daddy. I wonder where that mocha brown came from?"

"Well, Michelle isn't all that light of an individual. I am sure he got his color from her side of the family."

"Whelp come on in the house. Let me take the baby and hold him while you pray a little. Is that alright?"

I looked at Frank wondering why Pastor Jones would even fathom dealing with a newborn. Not that preachers didn't hold babies, I was just being a little overprotective.

"I think he will be okay, Pastor. Thanks anyway." I had already become attached and didn't want anyone to touch him besides his biological mother.

———

After prayer ended, I needed to find a spot to change Micah's soiled diaper. We walked down the hallway considering offices and classrooms trying to find a perfect space to do so.

"Don't you take that baby nowhere else but into Missy's office. She scrubs that office down every day with Clorox. Especially after the murder, so I know he will be alright in there.

Take him in the study and change him, gal," Pastor Jones demanded, observing our every move.

He walked with us into Missy's study plopping down on her leather sofa. We used a side chair for changing putting a blanket under the baby.

"You gonna be alright gal, with that baby? I know it takes some getting used to but you look so nervous holding him," he said.

"Nervous? I know it's hard to imagine me with a child Pastor but I am learning as I go. I am enjoying this experience that's for sure." I got misty-eyed just thinking about it as Frank leaned over and kissed me on the forehead for comfort. He had become a true superhero to me and would amp up like the Incredible Hulk if anyone dared to mess with me. I didn't have to envy Missy and Beanie anymore, I now had my own love story to write.

"I know it's hard for Michelle to be without him though. I hope she can keep herself together. I sure do hate that she has to eventually leave him and go to prison. Got to make sure she prayed up every day."

"Yes. I'm confident that she will get through this with a breeze. Eighteen months isn't as bad as five years. I believe God that she will get stronger and stronger throughout the transition."

"Well, look at God. Natalia Freemon is talking Godly talk. You have come a long way gal." He patted me on my shoulder.

The office windows were wide opened as we enjoyed a cool and refreshing breeze that seeped through the replaced curtains.

We heard a rattling noise outside and tried to figure out where it was coming from. The sounds reminded me of cans being dragged on the back of a car during a tailgate celebration.

I grabbed the baby, snapping the Velcro of his pamper tight as we all drew closer to the window.

Olivia Wallace pulled up to the church grounds, leaped out of that same red Ford truck with red gasoline cans, and bags of paper. Bruises remained all over her face from her Briar Creek beat down.

She walked to the back of the vehicle pulling out two more gas cans full of petroleum.

"What is she doing?" I asked picking up the baby and rocking him back and forth.

"It doesn't look like it's about to be anything, good babe. Let's get out of here." Frank said with alarm picking up the baby's belongings.

We ran down the hallway swiftly with the baby bag bouncing on Frank's back. We could smell the gasoline lingering throughout the church. Pastor Jones didn't leave right away as he yelled at the top of his lungs out of the window.

♪"You are the craziest woman on earth you know that Liv? Put that gas down before you blow up this building."

"Won't happen today Henry. No money, no church."

"Have you lost your mind woman? You know this is my mama's church. You destructive whoremonger, you."

Once he noticed that she wasn't listening he called into his blue tooth clearing the building. The five guards ran down the hall frantically clearing every room.

"Let's go people. Prayer is over. Let's go. Everyone out."

We made it to the walkway watching her pour every drop of liquid into all the garden beds that surrounded the windows. She talked out loud to herself putting the emptied cans back onto the truck.

"I don't know who told them that I was just going to go away without my money. They make me do things. They make me do crazy things," she said bunching up paper.

We walked into the open field of the church and dialed 911 as she continued to pour more gas. She reached into her pocket and pulled out a cigarette lighter. The pieces of paper were attached to the flames as she threw them down into every flower bed. Lighting up the pieces of paper seemed to give her joy.

"Oh my God." I had my hands over my mouth.

"Olivia *stop*. What are you doing? Lord help us, Jesus." Pastor

Jones threw up his hands and bent down touching his knee out of breath. "My arthritis can't take all of this. Don't do this to us. I will give you the money. Please. Don't do this." He howled in pain.

She continued talking to her group of imaginary friends and was totally lost in her imagination. She was in a zone that only one hundred thousand dollars could get her out of.

"They got me fighting folks, threatening folks, and now burning up the property. All that man had to do was give me my money."

She bent down, jumbling up more paper, leaves, and bark used to decorate the flower beds. The flames inched slowly up the bricks as she plopped down more items. She flicked her lighter again with her other hand on her tiny hips.

Pastor Jones rushed her like a defensive end football player and knocked her down to the ground. Once he realized how far the flames had gotten, he sobbed uncontrollably. He leaped over the walkway kicking the flower beds away from the church but it was too late. The flames rose high over the first-floor windows with a crackling sound that grew louder and louder.

"Are you crazy?" He jumped up and tried to stomp out the flames but nothing worked. Once the inferno circled around the building he yanked her again onto the grass putting his hand around her head trying to shake the evil spirit out of her. "Die demon! Die."

' She looked at him with dull eyes pushing his arms away with impetus strength. "Look at those flames sweet thang. They sure are up there, aren't they? The building is lighting up like it's Independence Day."

Pastor Jones dropped his hands down to his side, waddled in the grass, and cried nonstop. She looked back at us and waved as the flames were out of control with smoke coming out of every window. Our church, our foundation, our refuge was now being condemned by the devil herself.

Fire trucks were in motion. We all covered our mouths from the unbearable smoke. I tucked the baby away inching farther away from the building. But I was still close enough to see and hear the two of them while they sat in the grass. Olivia sat laughing while Pastor Jones had a touch of Missy's infamous meltdowns rubbing his arms and screaming loudly.

"You're never going to get away with this Olivia." He shouted. He kicked his feet up and down on the grass like a toddler realizing there was nothing more he could do.

She stood up holding a phone in her hand and waving it around in the air. Music played that we could barely hear. She then went to her truck, turned it on, and the same song was amplified thru woofer speakers that stood up in the back of the trunk.

MC Hammer's song, *Turn this Mutha Out* amplified out of the truck as she danced in circles to the beat.

She looked over and shouted, "I want to see your God fix all of this now, suckers."

She continued to dance jiggling up and down with sarcasm. She bounced around demonstrating the *Wop* looking ready for the *Soul Train* line. The music was louder than a 1970's block party being played on what was considered holy grounds.

Pastor Jones looked as if he had enough with his forehead creased. His qualms about the matter showed but he had no power to stop any of it. We stepped even further away now in the parking lot as the smoke became unbearable. The firemen swarmed the premises working hard trying to save the monumental building.

Pastor Jones moped pulling strands of grass from the roots and throwing it back down in shock. The flames pushed through the chimney of the building as long ladders stretched high swinging several uniformed men in the air.

The strong brick structure now looked like it was made of paper. The church known as Mt. Zion Holiness Church was no longer the bright and eye-catching church that could be seen from the highway. Soon and very soon it was going to be a pile of ashes. No prayer or holy oil could stop the massive devastation that Olivia Wallace caused. It was no need to continue to stand around especially with a newborn. We tucked the baby down in the car seat, got in our car, and drove away in tears. My mind was blown.

The flames continued as I cocked my head looking at the side mirrors.

TWENTY-SEVEN

MISSY

It was Sunday once again. Since Mt. Zion could not have service, everyone decided to meet up at Daddy's house. I was happy to see all my extended family gather around as we sat under a large pine tree in his big backyard. The trees shaded us from the sun while catching up with family and friends.

But when Michelle walked in, my happy spirit switched gears. She carried the baby and sat right across from me. I didn't understand why anyone would expect me to act normal around her. This entire situation wasn't Godly or normal and I wished that everyone would except that fact that not only is she a liar but a killer too. I just couldn't seem to catch a break from all the church drama.

Daddy wore a mask of worry across his face. It was obvious

he was overwhelmed but it was also obvious that the board meeting yesterday broke him completely down. Mother Smithfield was the ringleader and made sure that the entire board agreed to kick him off effective immediately. He still had the same look he carried yesterday when he walked out of the conference room with sweat drops pouring down his nostrils.

He played it off well. He couldn't stop talking about the entire scene during the fire and gave full details. He especially emphasized how Olivia had the audacity to shake her rump while tarnishing his legacy.

"Did anyone watch WRAL this morning?" I asked.

"Yea I did," Natalia responded. "Olivia was arrested for arson shortly after the fire. Did you know that, Pastor Jones?"

He looked surprised. "Nah, I didn't. But that didn't mean much, arresting her wasn't going to change the fact that the church was down to small pieces of rocks and soot. Father, God." He rubbed his beard.

The others huddled around like a family again as Natalia sat rocking Micah in and out of his sleep. Michelle was finally finished with passing him around the table for everyone to get a glimpse of his chinky eyes and round face. I couldn't be mean to the baby. It wasn't his fault that he existed. But I didn't want to touch him. He was a cute little thing, but holding him like the others was not my goal in life.

✎ Natalia paused as her phone chimed *Wave My Flag* by Mary Mary as the ringtone. She looked down at the caller ID.

"It's Duke Hospital. I wonder why they are calling on a Sunday? Do you want to take the call, Michelle? I am sure it's about the baby."

"Put it on speaker phone." Michelle was too busy preparing a bottle of milk.

"Hello"

"Yes, is this Ms. Hanks?" "Yes, it is."

"This is Doctor Ellis from Duke Hospital. How are you today?" "I am doing well. How's it going Doc?"

"Well, we got the newborn screening back. Sorry that I am calling on a Sunday. It's not my normal protocol. But I need you to come to the hospital tomorrow so that I can speak to you about something important."

"Is something wrong with my baby?"

I blew my breath. I was tired of seeing and hearing this baby. Everything circled around this baby. I anticipated her date to leave and serve her time. She needed to be under the jail. I just couldn't move past it all.

"Yes, but it is nothing alarming so don't worry. I remember you mentioning that you will be leaving soon so we need to discuss this as soon as possible. Can you come in tomorrow at 9 o'clock?"

"Yes, I can be there."

"Great. See you then."

"I wonder what that is about?" Natalia said.

Pastor Jones glanced over. "We can all go to support you gal. I'm sure you could use the company."

"That would be nice Pastor."

I hope that baby don't have to suffer due to her lies. He's the innocent one around here. But it never fails, a lie will always come full circle.

TWENTY-EIGHT

MICHELLE

Doctor's office...

"Ms. Hanks, we found some abnormalities with the test."

"What kind of abnormalities?"

"Micah's blood work determined that he has a rare blood disease that attacks babies from birth throughout their toddler years. We want to keep him overnight and find the right dosage of medications for him. This will give us the opportunity to take more tests. Some children grow out of this before preschool. While others may suffer until the age of seven. It all depends on his immune system."

"Okay." My eyes locked with Natalia. Her face squinted as if she was having second thoughts about taking on such a responsibility.

"So how do we care for a baby with this issue?" Natalia asked.

"Well, it's a rare disease and we don't have all the answers for cases like this. It won't end his life but it will require much attention to his needs."

"Sure, what is this rare disease called, Doc?" I asked.

"We are not sure. All we know is based upon other children we have seen with this, it is hereditary. Without knowing all the facts, I cannot give a diagnosis just yet."

"Wow." Natalia sat back in the chair.

"Do you know of anything in your past Michelle that was hereditary that wasn't noted in your files?" Doctor Ellis mumbled.

"Well, I am anemic but that is about it."

Natalia, Frank, Missy, Beanie, and Pastor Jones remained silent to the point where you could hear a pin drop. I was surprised to see Missy show up but then I realized she probably only tagged along because pastor Jones needed help driving since his blood pressure skyrocketed since the fire. It's not like he couldn't ride with someone else. I was pretty sure fifty percent of her appearance was sheer nosiness. She didn't want to show it but I knew deep down, she still cared.

"What about Tommy? Did he have a blood issue?" Missy

spoke with hesitation with her chest heaving.

Doctor Ellis looked at me out of the corner of his eye. "Well, Ms. Hanks, I don't know if you remember this but the brother of the deceased requested a blood test be done to prove the relationship of the baby. You agreed to that before the baby arrived and now that he is here we discovered…"

"What did you discover Doc?" Natalia sat up at attention, squirming in her seat.

"Mr. Arnold is not related to Micah."

"Excuse me? That is impossible." I said avoiding eye contact.

Missy started fanning herself and Pastor Jones plopped his hands on his knees looking down at the ground.

Natalia stood, still taking deep breaths.

What in the world is going on around here?

Knowing Natalia, she was going to make sure the Doctor answered all her questions. She wouldn't dare let him leave anything out. Especially if I was expecting for her to be accountable for taking care of a sick child. Her voice became an octave higher. She said, "What is going on Doc?"

"Calm down Hun." Frank scooted beside her grabbing her hand.

"I need to know. I didn't sign up for this." Beads of sweat covered her cheeks.

Natalia looked directly at me. "You have some serious explaining to do young lady. I thought we surpassed all the nonsense. Spill it." She poked her finger in the air ready to go in full accusatory mode. "Michelle, I need you to look me in my eyes and tell me who the father of this baby is. If you can bring us all here to support you then you can tell us all what is going on too."

"What?" I couldn't believe she asked the question as I moved up to the edge of my seat.

"I know you know who the father is... if it isn't Tommy, then stop with all this cat and mouse. I wondered what was up with that dark brown complexion anyway." Natalia looked as if her heart was bursting inside her chest.

Everyone turned to Micah eyeballing his brown glow.

"So just because Tommy is light-skinned, doesn't mean it's not his baby, Natalia. Are you kidding me right now?" I yelled.

Missy slumped down into the seat. "More drama. Here we go again. I knew I should have stayed in my bed. I am so sick of you all." Her extremities shook all over.

"You okay?" I asked. The last thing we needed was for her anxiety to unleash while trying to figure out what was going on with my baby.

Her feet tapped, her cries roared, she hopped up out of her seat and clasped her hands together. "PASTOR HENRY

CEPHEUS JONES..."

He looked up stupidly. "It's Daddy to you, gal. Don't be out here being disrespectful."

"Huh?" Beanie conveyed.

"Huh?" Frank added.

Missy couldn't stop panting as she started gasping for air. "Daddy... You're the only one I know on this earth who had a rare blood disease as a child. Mother Smithfield said something about it after that board meeting where she fussed you out."

"You heard that too huh? You need to be a private eye, not a pastor, gal."

"Oh God. Oh God, so it is true. Nooooo... Nooooo... Daddy? Is that... is that your baby?" She pointed at the baby as all six set of eyes ogled over apprehensively.

"You better start talking, Pastor Jones... If it's your seed, you will definitely take him home with you while Michelle is in prison. I don't want any part of this mess."

My eyes zeroed in on him while his eyes zeroed in on me. Then all eyes zeroed in on Micah.

To be continued...

EPILOGUE

The Drama Continues...

Yellow tape circled the 6500-square foot building. Signs that said private property stuck in the muddy grass and were visible from the busy street. The dawn of the morning allowed the sun to crack into the surface of the sky, showing a tinge of light.

Although the building had been tarnished, the center frame of the structure had been saved. There was still access to offices and the dining hall with light treading across the broken glass from the windows.

Olivia Wallace tiptoed into the building with her brother in search of the safe that was tucked away in the Pastor's study. They carried flashlights, rubber gloves, and rubber shoe coverings not wanting to leave any form of evidence. They stumbled, jerked, and rocked around the cement foundation that was once a linoleum floor.

"We got to get that safe Larry. He had one-hundred-dollar bills stacked all in that thing."

Larry moved around like a pro maneuvering his body so that he wouldn't bump against any of the objects that flew office shelves from the fire.

"Liv, I shole' hope you telling the truth about this one. I could use the cash." He rubbed his fingers together anticipating the thought of being loaded with the church's money. He carried a large tool bag on his back filled with a shovel, hammer, and pliers. He didn't know how to crack a safe, but he was gonna do whatever it took to make it happen.

"It was over here in this area." Olivia felt her way looking down at the floor.

"Sis. Look... I think that's it over there."

In the corner of the room was the black mini safe.

They pried, banged, and pounced on the top and side of it with   the tools.

After several minutes of banging the door, the safe cracked open.

They jumped up and down excited about finding the mystery jackpot.

"You did it this time Liv. I'll be darn. We're about to come up from the gutter and into the penthouse."

*Larry danced around singing *Just Got Paid* by Johnny Kemp. He pulled out a pair of safety glasses from his bag clearing all the residue off the door frame. As he inched closer to pull the door outward, there was a brown paper bag placed in the center.

"That's it. *That's it*," Olivia screamed. She reached her hands in and pulled out several plastic grocery bags. "It must be at the bottom."

"It better be." Her brother looked down peeping in the bag.

She had gotten to the last piece of plastic that was left inside the paper bag. It had a note stuck down with glue.

She pulled it out read it aloud:

This is what my God can do. He can tell me to go and get my money immediately after a fire, just so I can keep all of it away from you.

From the Pastor that don't owe you jack!

Olivia slumped over howling with her raspy voice. "This man has cursed me. I know he has. There is no way I can be so unlucky." She kicked and screamed, banging her foot hard on the safe. Olivia grabbed it, wincing as it throbbed in sheer agony.

Her brother shook his head and put all his tools back into his bag. "I guess that is what happens when you don't have God on your side. Look like these folks got God, Jesus, the Holy Spirit and all of heaven protecting them."

They exited the building with only the tool bag they entered in with...

ABOUT THE AUTHOR

Teresa B. Howell

Teresa B. Howell was raised in Boston, Massachusetts. She is an educator, mentor, and advocate for students with special needs. Born and raised in the church, it was fitting to tell her story. She currently resides in Durham, North Carolina with her husband and children.

That Church Life 1 & 2 is available on Amazon.com and Barnesandnoble.com.

For more information or updates:
www.teresabhowell.com

CPSIA information can be obtained
at www.ICGtesting.com
Printed in the USA
LVOW10s2002020318

568482LV00012B/646/P